THE CRAIGSLIST MURDERS

THE

CRAIGSLIST MURDERS

A NOVEL

BRENDA CULLERTON

The Craigslist Murders

First Melville House Printing: January 2011

Melville House Publishing
145 Plymouth Street
Brooklyn, New York 11201
mhpbooks.com

ISBN: 978-1-61219-019-8

Printed in the United States of America
1 2 3 4 5 6 7 8 9 10

Library of Congress Cataloging-in-Publication Data
Cullerton, Brenda.
The Craigslist murders: a novel / Brenda Cullerton.
p. cm.
ISBN 978-1-61219-019-8
1. Murder--Fiction. 2. Rich people--Fiction. 3. Manhattan (New York, N.Y.)--Fiction. I. Title.
PS3603.U584C73 2011
813'.6--dc22

2010049601

With the exception of references to BBS (Birkin Bag Syndrome), PJNS (Private Jet Neck Syndrome), and the contents of a Golden Globe swag bag, this is a work of fiction. Any resemblance to actual events or persons, living or dead, is entirely coincidental.

For Richard and Rachel

"Men are not punished for their sins, but by them."

—E. G. HUBBARD

1

AUGUST

Charlotte had been getting away with murder for years. Most interior decorators—desecrators, she called them—got away with murder. Her killings usually came in the form of modest mark-ups and kickbacks. Modest compared to her colleagues, anyway. It was unbelievable. Forget the famous $6,000 Tyco shower curtain. That was old news. Yesterday, some dealer at an art show in Dallas had called her about a nice pair of $25,000 vinyl-sculptured, light switches. But enough about work, she couldn't wait to shut this girl up. A nail-thin, Nordic blonde, she was jabbering away on her iPhone to some friend who had just harvested her eggs.

Privacy and God. Both dead! Charlotte muttered, as she pretended not to listen and scanned the room. The French ultramarine blue walls, yellow ochre trims, and low chrome couches were nice. But *whoa!* The lamp? It looked like some kind of grotesquely bloated sea urchin. Something that might sting you when you turned it on. The wall near the picture window was covered with photographs of the girl's geriatric husband, mingling with the city's powers-that-be, and showing off his lovely new acquisition. The "acquisition," now puckering her lips and blowing kisses into the phone, was wearing more logos than a NASCAR driver.

For Charlotte, logos were the symbol of an insidious form of identity theft. The theft began as early as infancy when her clients swaddled their newborns in itty bitty blankets of "F" for Fendi cashmere. *F for all F'ed up*, Charlotte had thought the last time she ooh'ed and ahh'ed over a baby in a $3,000 Corsican Paris iron crib on New York's Upper East Side. Charlotte herself loved beautiful things. Some of them even had logos. But everything she owned had an emotional presence; something that spoke of her own hunger to be understood, her passion for beauty itself.

The delicately painted porcelain cup balanced on her knee, for example. It was Herend. She'd checked. Herend had a history. It bore the hallmark of the Hungarian royal family. Charlotte imagined that this girl associated Hungary, like Turkey, with something to eat. Pulling her mass of long red hair tightly back from her face, Charlotte stuck a pen in the knot to hold it, and focused on the mission ahead.

"So who gave you the bracelet?" she asked as the girl pressed "End Call" and placed the phone on the coffee table.

"Yes, well … an old boyfriend in Chicago gave it to me when I graduated from Joliet Junior College," she replied. "It's Bulgari. See? And this is the *Tour Eiffel.* He collected all the charms on a trip we took to Europe before I started modeling."

"How charming," Charlotte replied. "Pun intended, of course." Blowing on her tea, she'd cringed at the French words "Tour Eiffel." It was so affected, like when people raved about "Ha*b*ana" or "Bar*th*elona." The sharp cramp in her abdomen forced her to take a deep breath. Was it the girl's smug, vacuous smile? Or the way she kept flashing her grotesquely oversized canary yellow diamond ring?

"The problem is, my husband doesn't really appreciate its sentimental value. And I'd rather not have it in the house as a reminder, you know?"

"Well, you must love him very much," Charlotte said, feeling queasy. "And where is your husband now?"

For the next twenty minutes, Charlotte listened to her recite the guy's whole resume, including his nine million dollar Christmas bonus, while also sniveling on about how long he'd been gone (five days) and how "awesomely happy" they were as a couple.

What is this sob story about missing husbands? Charlotte wondered. *He isn't Daniel Pearl, for Christ's sake. He's some ancient I-banker screwing interns on a business trip.* The more the girl whined and the more she fiddled with her enormous ring, the more angry Charlotte became. Her teeth chattered. She shivered. People always talk about the heat of anger. For Charlotte, it was the cold. She was so cold. She even looked to see if her own skin had stuck to the fire poker before rolling it back up in her bright yellow yoga mat.

Much like her encounter with the divorcee months earlier—a woman unloading a case of vintage Dom—a couple of heavy blows to the head from behind was all it took to send the girl whimpering to the floor. After eight years of Pilates, Charlotte was pretty pumped. She'd hit her so hard the first time, the poker had vibrated in her hand. She'd had to tighten her grip. It was weird, the way the girl seemed to drift down, *lazily*, like leaves falling from a tree, into a sitting position on the floor.

But the mechanics of killing bored Charlotte. It was the small, seemingly insignificant details that moved her. They were so preternaturally vivid: the dribble of bright red seeping into a blond sisal carpet, the darker splatter, the smears, on a shiny chartreuse chintz pillow, the pale pink sugary residue in the bottom of the teacup that matched the color of the girl's nails. It was surreal, this saturation of color. Like being trapped in the frames of an Almodovar movie. This vividness was precisely what Charlotte enjoyed most about these moments. It made her feel so acutely, so exquisitely, *alive.*

Being a bit of a neat freak helped a lot with the tidying up after. The swiping of surfaces with her Handi Wipes, the change of exercise leggings, the removal of the bracelet and the cup. (The cup would make a lovely new addition to her collection of mismatched quality china.) By the time Charlotte had completed these rituals, her cramps had gone, and the girl's bleating cries had finally stopped.

It wasn't until she got home that she noticed the blood on the collar of her cream silk shirt. "God damn it!" she said, furiously scrubbing away at the stain and leaving it to soak in the kitchen sink. She also washed her yoga mat in the laundry area and polished the poker (a filthy job) before replacing it next to the fireplace. The scalding hot rainforest shower had never felt so good.

Unlike her mother's spartan, functional bathrooms, Charlotte believed in the "sanctuary" concept. So what if people laughed at her silver-leaf tiles, the fuchsia pink egg-shaped tub, and her $15,000 Toto toilet? Nobody knew about clean like the Japanese. It was a cultural obsession, wasn't it? And there was something so soothing about the toilet's water wand, the warm air dryer, the heated seat.

"Jesus! It does everything but kiss your ass!" one of her clients' husbands had exclaimed, after she'd installed three Totos in their brownstone.

At fifteen grand a pop, she wasn't surprised to see that another had somehow "fallen off the truck" and found its way into her loft. Volume discounts were how her business worked. You spent thousands, tens of thousands, buying merchandise for clients from a vendor and the vendor owed you. Period. Hell, she knew interior designers who had furnished entire country homes, right down to their Sherle Wagner gold-plated faucets, from volume discounts.

The press didn't report the murder until two days later. Skimming the headline inside the *Post*: "Model, Homemaker Murdered!" the article also mentioned that the 25-year-old "victim" (*Fashion victim, maybe*, Charlotte had snorted to herself) had died of blunt-trauma injuries after being hit in the head with an unknown object.

Even if police checked the girl's e-mail correspondence and made the connection between Craigslist and buyers visiting the apartment, Charlotte wasn't worried. She'd set the whole thing up under a pseudonym on a public-access computer at Kinko's.

2

FOUR WEEKS LATER

Taking a tiny sip from her glass of chilled Stag's Leap, Charlotte entered the museum's vast new atrium. The immensity of the space left her breathless, giddy. The ceilings that seemed to soar up forever, the 80-foot sheet of single-pane glass overlooking the gardens, the marble and sea-foam slate floors. It reminded her of the first time she'd ever set foot in a mosque, the glory of all that uninterrupted space. What a spectacular backdrop for tonight's dinner.

People who say money reeks have never smelled real money, she thought, while checking out the intimate groupings of snow-white, linen-covered tables. No, the money made by trustees of this museum had been so thoroughly laundered; all that was left was the discreet scent of Creed. *How ironic*, Charlotte sniggered. Most of the men in this room had done such unspeakably dirty things to amass their billions. But they all looked so pristine, so immaculately clean.

They lived clean, too. Smiling coyly at the male waiter and nibbling on a bit of billowy puff pastry, Charlotte thought some more about this generation of freshly-minted money—a generation that did everything but spend and exercise in moderation. They didn't smoke. They didn't drink. They barely ate. The women were so self-consumed, there was nothing left of them but skin and bones. Faux blondes with Sulka-smooth faces and foreheads as shiny as Granny Smith apples, they all looked the same. *More identity theft*, Charlotte thought as she waved to a knot of women clustered near the bar. Some were former clients and others, friends of clients.

Back in the flush of her "brilliant, breakthrough success" (who could forget a rave like that from *Architectural Digest*?) Charlotte had been invited to lunch by a new client.

"I don't do lunch," she'd replied, offhandedly. When the woman's personal assistant phoned the next morning to cancel her contract, Charlotte panicked. The remark could have killed her career. She hadn't meant to sound haughty. She simply had better things to do. Like work. Now, she lunched twice a week. As Charlotte continued to survey the room, she noticed a guy staring at her, pointing at her shoes. What the hell was his name?

Even at thirty-seven years old, Charlotte knew that she was one of the best-looking women there. It wasn't just the shoes—satin slippers, actually. She was wearing one red and one black from separate pairs that she'd picked up on sale at the Liwan boutique in Paris. And it wasn't just her clothes—a beautiful old Beene shrug of hand-sewn red paillettes and a blissfully simple black jersey jumpsuit. It was the pale, creamy skin, emerald green eyes, and shock of fiery red hair that encircled her face like a halo—"the halo from hell," some hideous ex-business partner had once called it.

Charlotte had a lot of ex-partners. *But this isn't why women are staring at me tonight*, she thought. *They're jealous.*

Style, like happiness, can't be bought. Not real style. And Charlotte had it. "Elle sait faire" she'd overheard Caroline say about her to friends. Considering Caroline was the chicest French dealer in town, this was quite a compliment.

Oh right! Now she recognized the guy. It was the "hedgie" who worked in Greenwich Village.

"That's short for hedge fund, dear," the guy had said with a wink when she sat down next to him at some interminable private school auction last year.

"Wow!" Charlotte had replied, her eyes as round as saucers. "I think I've heard of those."

Half her clients were married to hedge fund guys. Where did this moron think she'd been for the past ten years? As she recalled, the auction highlights included a $22,000 winning bid for "A Bedtime Story and Tuck In" by one of the school's kindergarten teachers and a $42,000 bid for a cute patchwork quilt made by second graders. She couldn't wait to get home. Christ! And there he was again tonight, bobbing up and down in the crowd, saluting her. What was with the saluting?

"Hi there!" Lunging in to plant a wet kiss on her cheek, the guy spilled half a glass of wine on his pants. "Remember me?"

"The hedgie," Charlotte replied, politely passing him a cocktail napkin. "Short for hedge fund, right?"

"You got it, baby!" he said, blotting his thigh with one hand while grabbing another glass from a passing waiter. "Name's Judd."

For the next fifteen minutes, Judd tore off on a verbal "test drive" in his brand-new, fully-loaded $350,000 Maybach 57s.

Charlotte had only seen these pimped out chauffeur-driven sedans double-parked on the street. She didn't even have a driver's license. So by the time, he'd revved his way through twelve cylinder power packs, maximum torque of 1000 nm (whatever the fuck that was), rear aprons, and anthracite Alcantra, she'd felt like a piece of roadkill. He then switched to the subject of his fortieth birthday party.

"Did I tell you I paid for the Stones, Charlotte?" (*Yes, about ninety times,* she'd muttered to herself.)

"Eight million, but I got to sing with Mick!"

"What a treat for Mick," she said.

"Who says you can't get no satisfaction, huh?" he added, poking her playfully in the ribs, as she turned to speak with the plump "too-tan-from-a-can-man" sidling in on her left.

"I wouldn't eat that if I were you," the man said, snidely, pointing to the slender stalk of spring asparagus on the tip of her toothpick.

"Why not?" she was fool enough to ask. "I love asparagus!"

"Well, I happen to import 80% of America's asparagus from Peru."

Do you, now? Charlotte whispered to herself. *How absolutely fascinating.*

"We fumigate the shit out of it with bleach and fungicide before we ship it. It's not great for the prostate," he chuckled, eyeing his private parts.

"Guess I'm glad I don't have a prostate," Charlotte answered, swallowing the stalk in a single bite.

Now where the hell was Philip? People were being corralled toward the tables at the back of the atrium. Ah! Finally. Standing on tiptoes, she watched as a sleek silver-haired man slithered his way through the crowd towards her. *How I pity your wife,* Charlotte thought to herself. Philip, known to all but his wife, Vicky, as "Phil Phil" (the "Philandering Philanthropist") was heir to one of the city's biggest real estate fortunes. Charlotte had managed to keep him at arm's length for years and had come tonight only as favor to his wife.

Vicky, her oldest friend, was off in Aspen, dealing with last minute contract changes for the third condo. That was the other weird thing about the really rich: Money was as meaningless to them as death, or physical death, anyway, was to terrorists. Most of her clients, for instance, didn't even bother to pay for health insurance. (Who needed the hassle of health insurance with billions in the bank?) But she'd never met a single one who didn't need just a tiny bit more.

"Un poquito mas! Un poquito mas!" she heard the hedge fund guy shouting over and over again to the befuddled waiter, attempting to nudge his way past with a trayful of empty glasses. The kid wasn't even Hispanic. "Hielo! Hielo!" he repeated, rattling the ice cubes in his glass. But yeah... Whether it was ice cubes, condos, cows, (beg your pardon, *cattle*), shoes, or money, they always needed just a little more.

"God! Gorgeous bracelet, Charlotte." She flinched. Philip had somehow drifted in from behind her. With one hand snaked around her waist, he lifted her wrist for a closer look. "Vicky's been begging for one. I should have known you were the woman to ask. So where did you get it?"

"Craigslist," she said, giving her wrist a shake.

"You're kidding," he replied, utterly dumbfounded. "It's

eighteen karat," he spluttered. "And it's solid. I can hear the clunk."

"Don't look so shocked," Charlotte replied, slipping her arm through his. "It comes with quite a story, too."

As Philip guided her, oh-so adroitly, toward their table, she fumed. *So typical! Dismissing yet another world he knows nothing about.* Craigslist wasn't just some secondhand, online shopping bazaar. It was a compulsion; a vital, visceral connection to the city, a connection that was changing people's lives. But what did Philip know of change? Like most men, he probably hated change. (Unless, of course, the change involved a new wife.)

He was beaming as he pulled out her chair. "Close enough to the dais for you, Charlotte?" Unfolding her napkin, she prepared to endure another profoundly shallow, short, conversation with her host. There was grit in the arugula.

"You have no idea," Philip said as she rootled through the salad in search of a sun-dried tomato or a pignolia nut, "but new money is ruining, just ruining, *my* Anguilla! I mean, we may have to go to Lyford after Christmas."

Appearing suitably aghast, Charlotte buttered a roll. Poor Philip. Forced to book a $40,000 week at one of the most luxurious clubs in the Caribbean. But it amused her, how he used the possessive pronoun when referring to Anguilla. As if he owned the entire island. When he turned to his left to chat up some magnificent young Russian, she smirked. A titaness of downtown real estate, Charlotte had recently heard that the girl had bought the biggest piece of beachfront property left on "his" Anguilla.

She was admiring the pale pink fat and flesh of her

tuna—it was so silky, so light, it seemed to evaporate in her mouth—when the man on her left burped into his napkin. Eyes nailed to his plate, he flushed with embarrassment.

"Not exactly Bumble Bee, is it?" she said, rescuing him with her most ravishing smile. *He couldn't be a day over 23*, she thought.

"No, I guess not." He shifted his gaze from his plate to somewhere near her neck. "I've never tasted anything like it."

"Forgive me. I haven't introduced myself," she said, sticking out her hand. "I'm Charlotte Wolfe." They shook.

"And I'm Peter Winthrop. Assistant curator in Islamic art."

Passing him a generous spoonful of her own tuna, she asked herself how an assistant curator had landed so close to the dais. "It's tuna belly," she added as the boy forked up another mouthful. "I have a friend who buys it on online from the Philippines. Sixty bucks a can, if you can imagine."

His eyes bulged. She didn't mention that Vicky used to have her cook pack it up in sandwiches for her kid's school lunches.

He grinned. "Nothing's too good for our trustees." Pausing for a moment, he picked up a corner of the tablecloth as Charlotte looked at him, curiously.

"I'm not sneaking a look at your legs," he explained. "It's your slippers. Everybody loves them."

"Ah! Two different colored slippers. It's one of my signatures," she winked.

While Peter polished off his extra portion of fish and fingerling potatoes, Charlotte crossed her ankles beneath the table and wondered how Vicky was doing in Aspen. Friendships, like marriages, took years to fall apart. She knew that. But Charlotte liked being precise. She had to be precise. The business of interior design depended as much on precision as it did on the imagination. Measuring the exact dimensions of everything from furniture to oddly-shaped windows, selecting the perfect tint of alabaster white marble from hundreds of samples at the Cararra quarry in Italy, mixing and matching from thousands of different woods, tiles, and shades of paints and fabric. This is why she wished that she could pinpoint, precisely, when it had all started to go so disastrously wrong with Vicky; when her role had switched from that of trusted friend and confidante to something more along the lines of an unpaid personal assistant.

In college, Vicky had inspired an almost childlike sense of awe in Charlotte. Slender and exquisitely feminine (versus savagely female which is what she had now become), there had been a nonchalant grace, a sort of effortless splendor, about her that made her seem both innocent and seductive. Even her awkwardness was alluring.

Startled out of her reverie by a burst of prolonged applause, Charlotte rose to her feet with the crowd. They were cheering the gnome-like giant of finance at the podium. Charlotte could see his spittle as he stammered through the beginning of his speech. Returning, gratefully, to her own musings, she smiled. Vicky's adoption of her as official best friend had been marked with the gift of two cashmere sweaters. They were hand-me-downs from her father. One was a pale shade of beige, "The color of a baby fawn," Vicky had said. And the other, a deep emerald green, "To match your wonderful eyes."

Charlotte still wore the green one around the house. The sleeves had unraveled and there were gaping holes beneath the armpits. As worn-out and frayed as their friendship, Charlotte had neither the heart nor the courage to throw it out. Throwing it out would imply that she had abandoned her youth; that she'd given up on the pleasures of being needed. This is what Vicky had taught her. That being needed was almost as good as being loved.

The rattle of dinner plates as waiters cleared the table and refilled water glasses jolted her back into the present. Eyeing her nervously, the curator scribbled something on the back of his menu and slid it in her direction. She peered at the tiny, crabbed handwriting.

"May I ask you for a drink later?" it said.

She scribbled back, "Maybe next time!"

Charlotte would never have dreamed of taking the boy up on his offer. But at thirty-seven, she still appreciated the gesture. Waiting for Philip's cue to leave, (she'd agreed to join him only if he promised that they'd escape before dessert) Charlotte tapped her foot. The cue came in the form of his hand, pawing her thigh. Placing her own hand gently on top of his, as if to stroke it, she proceeded to pinch the flesh so hard between her fingernails, he yelped.

"Ready to go?" Charlotte asked, sweetly.

As the curator stood up and gallantly handed over her sequin clutch, she caught Philip whispering into the ear of the Russian girl while pocketing her business card. Had the man no shame? She wanted to kick him. His secret was safe with Charlotte, of course. To tell Vicky would wound her pride. As bright and polished as the shiny shell of a ladybug, this thin veneer of pride was all that remained of the girl Charlotte had known in college. It had to be protected. And this was Charlotte's job. Not just with Vicky but with clients, too. *To protect and to serve*, she muttered to herself as Philip glad-handed his way towards the exit. *That's my motto. Just like the L.A. cops.*

3

It was 8:30 Monday morning and Charlotte was trawling through the List at a newscafe on Lower Broadway. The place was getting busy. Too busy. She didn't like the idea of strangers seeing what was on her screen. Not that it was dangerous. Thousands, maybe millions, of New Yorkers, surfed through the List every day. She just preferred to hunt alone. A teenage boy with huge wooden plugs in his earlobes sat sprawled in the chair next to her. The skin of the lobe had stretched so much, the flesh seemed to drip, like clocks in a Dali painting.

"Hey, lady," the boy said, tugging hard on his ear when he caught her staring. "You want the name of the guy put these in?"

Charlotte winced. "Sorry," she said, shifting her eyes back to the screen.

The boy continued tapping at his keyboard as she clicked on a posting in the Collectibles section of the List and chuckled.

"Outta here! Every stick of his louzy, rotton furniture!"

With the exception of the atrocious spelling, Charlotte could relate. When she'd been dropped by her ex-boyfriend Paul, she'd felt that same urge to dump every item in her house that he'd touched. Every item but the Dustbuster and the ring that he'd given her in Venice. Paul was a passive aggressive, self-serving, pretty boy who had happily moved on from the pittance he'd earned at Christies to a new job as a "decorative-arts advisor." They'd both had a good guffaw over that one. She clicked on a posting from Queens for a couch.

"Like new from the 17th century." The seller's mother (recently "deseized") had covered the couch in Saran Wrap. "So it never gets dirty." Earlier, she'd stumbled on a couple of other bizarre listings, too. One for a "Beautiful Clear Body Bag" and the other for a door that belonged to "Van Go!"

This is what had first attracted Charlotte to the List. Listening to all these voices, these stories that came from the hearts of the timid, the fearless, the rich, the poor, the misfits, the lying, the lonely. It was a kind of urban symphony. Like listening to the sounds of salsa, hip hop, jazz, and rock and roll that blared out from various cars lined up at red lights. At first, she'd stay up half the night, browsing and clicking, and e-mailing back and forth. It wasn't just the compulsive hunt for "victims" that drove her. It was her relationship with the List itself. It seemed almost human, the way it called out to her.

Then when the words became flesh; when she actually met the women who posted the listings, she grew even more addicted. Like those moments of intimacy shared by strangers on a long distance train ride, they opened themselves up to her, confessing to everything from abortions to cheating on and stalking their husbands. She felt like a Peeping Tom—an emotional voyeur.

She didn't always kill. Far from it. Sometimes, Charlotte simply used the List to satisfy her curiosity. It was fascinating, the journey through other people's homes. Especially when she was just a tourist; when it wasn't for work. The young woman with the Shabby Chic couch, for instance. Her husband had left her and she'd sat, weeping, beneath a gilt-leafed mirror in a ten-room apartment on 68th Street while Charlotte spring-tested the down pillows.

As the girl abandoned herself to convulsive waves of sobbing, her shoulders shuddering, her nose all red and veiny, Charlotte had reached out, impulsively, to touch her hand. *There's something almost voluptuous about her surrender*, she'd thought. Giving into grief was an extravagance—an extravagance that cost so little. And yet she knew so few who indulged in it. They took pills or got collagen shots, or shopped and jumped on a jet instead.

This was the other thing she'd learned after entering the life of the List. Even if many of these women had been deserted by their spouses or lovers or fired from their jobs, Charlotte discovered that she envied them in their despair. Broke, desperate, and ditching their possessions, they were gripped by the terror of new beginnings.

Years ago, every time she'd walked through the virgin stillness of a raw space, a space not yet born, she'd felt that same sweet terror, that exhilarating sense of expectation, of hope. For months, she'd carry the vision of its possibilities deep down inside her, bringing it slowly to life, feeling it kick, as she did her sketches, saturating walls with bright splashes of vivid color and accumulating the objects that gave her interiors such intimacy and warmth. But those years were long gone.

Charlotte's phone vibrated. *Damn!* She'd lost all sense of time. She always did when she browsed through the List. It was 9:30. Maybe she'd come back after dinner. There hadn't been a single posting from the Upper East Side, anyway. No one selling any of the high-end, logo'ed merchandise that made her eyes light up. Unloading expensive merchandise on Craigslist indicated a certain carelessness with money. The sort of carelessness that implied someone else had paid for it. Someone like a rich husband. Charlotte suddenly realized she was hungry.

As she logged off and shut down the computer, the guy with the wooden plugs winked at her. After paying at the counter and replacing her credit card in her wallet, she thought, again, of those years long gone. Years when the future had beckoned her with all of the feverish intensity and promise of a new lover. She was trapped now. Trapped in a space that felt as suffocatingly small and airless as the steel-clad, soundproofed panic rooms in which so many of the women she knew retreated to let off steam.

"It's the only place I feel safe enough to lose control," Vicky had explained. "To let go and really scream." They'd been having tea at the Four Seasons. The hair on Charlotte's neck had stood on end. She'd shivered. After climbing into the cocoon of her jet black Mercedes, Vicky had lowered the back seat window.

"I can't feel anything, Charlotte," she'd moaned. "Nothing ever happens to me."

Charlotte had made vague, reassuring noises while biting her tongue. *Nothing ever happens to the rich, Vicky*, a voice inside had wanted to shout. *Haven't you heard? It's like driving with air bags. There's always something to cushion the blows.*

4

"It's ridiculous, Anna. These women, they have everything, but they envy me."

Anna laughed. "Envy is all they know, my dear."

Setting out a single Porthault placemat, Charlotte rifled through the kitchen drawer, pulling out her favorite old hotel silver. It was a ritual. Just like these late Monday morning calls from Anna. She would gossip while Charlotte wolfed down an enormous breakfast. (Her appetite was another thing about Charlotte that drove her starving female clients crazy.)

"I'm single. I'm in debt up to my eyeballs," she said, her voice trailing off.

"Who isn't?" Anna replied, briskly. "Aside from your clients? Living beyond one's means is an art in New York. As for being single ... please do not let's go there."

"It's please don't go there, no let's." Charlotte said, gently correcting the slip. Anna's English was fluent. The occasional idiomatic mistake only added to her charms. And she was right. She was better off without Paul.

"You forget the most important thing, Charlotte. You have confidence."

Slathering a piece of toast with imported Dutch butter and jam, Charlotte sighed. "Not really. I just pretend."

"Two seconds, cara. Someone's on the other line..."

The toast was burnt. Punching the speaker button so that she could hear her friend when she returned to the line, Charlotte swept up a pile of charred crumbs. "The happiest cynics on earth." This is how Fellini described his fellow Italians. Anna fit that description to a tee. The Wop Wasp, which is what the designer, Bill Blass, had affectionately called her, was equally apt. An extraordinarily elegant Venetian antique dealer, Anna was the kind of woman other women dressed for. Charlotte was as enamored of her restraint, her perfect manners and quiet chic, as she was of her baroque-like outpourings of opinion and emotion. At sixty-seven years old, nothing surprised her.

She was also the only woman who seemed to appreciate Charlotte's gestures. Cutting off another slice of bread and sliding it in the toaster, Charlotte realized how much she looked forward to finding the small gifts at flea markets and Tepper auctions: gifts like old marbles, vintage Christmas ornaments, crystal-studded compacts from the '20s and gold-flecked beeswax candles. Anna was infatuated with all things that sparkled, things that caught the light and dazzled the eye. "Italy is defined by gestures," she would announce, giving Charlotte a quick kiss. "And you are a master of the grand gesture." Gazing at her reflection in the silvery surface of the toaster, Charlotte knew that the gifts were also a form of courtship; part of her timid but determined efforts to create a connection with Anna. It was complicated, making a new friend at her age. There were no reference points, no common history.

The pop of the toaster shattered the silence as Anna's voice returned to the line.

"Charlotte? I'm back. And just so you know... All real confidence begins with pretending."

"I'll keep that in mind, Anna. So what's new?"

"Cara! I cannot wait to tell you the latest story about Caroline. You are going to scream!"

"Lunch then?" Charlotte asked, steaming the milk beneath the nozzle of her new $1,000 coffee machine. "I'm looking for some Murano glass for my Russian client."

"Certo! We will meet at Boulud, eh? And ti giuro, my news will make the whole trip uptown worth it!"

"I doubt it, Anna. But I'll see you at noon."

"Bacione, bella. See you then."

Sitting at her kitchen table and soaking up the splendid river view, Charlotte took another sip from her cappuccino. The coffee machine had come "free" with her purchase of a ridiculously overpriced 19th century French commode. She'd recently acquired it from a young dealer for Pavel, her Russian client. After she'd admired it—the machine not the commode—in his shop, the dealer had sent it over as a "surprise" with a lovely note, complimenting her on her taste. "My taste for coffee?" she'd asked, smirking when she called to thank him. The piece itself had been so mercilessly restored only rappers and Russians like Pavel could love it.

Piling her dishes in the old Italian marble sink, Charlotte slowly ran her hands over its scarred, pitted surface. She'd bought the sink in Padua, probably the only time in her life she hadn't haggled like hell. The Italian dealer was so astounded, he'd asked her why.

"Because I like to imagine a mother washing dishes in it," she'd blushed. She was picturing the Italian farmhouse that she'd visited in the spring. This was after traveling over to check on a shipment of marble.

It was the sturdiness of the house that had nearly moved her to tears. There was no flash, nothing flimsy. Just thick plaster walls, heavy oak chairs, a great hearth, and smoothly worn tiled floors. Seated by her host at a long, wooden table, she'd sipped from a glass of rough red wine and watched his wife make the pasta. It was mesmerizing, the rhythm: cracking and separating the egg yolks, dropping them into peaks of soft white flour, folding and rolling the dough. *It was a rhythm born of ritual, tradition and memory*, Charlotte had thought wistfully.

Pointing towards the wall with her chin at the photographs of her three children, the woman seemed so infectiously happy, Charlotte was almost embarrassed. But this is why she'd forked over such an absurd price for the sink and even paid to have it shipped by air. She'd *needed* to have it near her, to be in touch with that kind of love.

The metamorphosis of Charlotte's loft from a nondescript white space into a tiny jewel box of extravagant color and texture had been her own labor of love. She'd lacquered the floors in a high gloss eggshell white and scattered them with bright sapphire, ruby and emerald threaded tribal rugs. The walls were painted in deep shades of Prince purple and amethyst, poppy red and black, and lapis. There were also floor-to-ceiling bookshelves in both the living room and bedroom.

Some people might have found the small book-filled painted rooms, claustrophobic. But Charlotte liked the feeling of being enclosed. When she pulled the heavy Italian brocade and velvet curtains tightly shut at night and heard the clunk of wooden rings on the long poles, the sound reminded her that she was safe. Anna, the only person other than Paul who had ever been invited inside, had been ecstatic when Charlotte offered a tour. "It's divine, cara. Like living inside a cozy embrace," she'd said.

Quickly checking the time while drying her Herend cup, Charlotte washed down the counter. She'd have a fast shower and review Darryl's sketches. Darryl, an up-and-coming fashion designer married to billions, had hired Charlotte to redo the library and five of the bedrooms in her new apartment on Park. There were some photos from a gallery in Chelsea that she'd promised to drop off, too. It was unreal. The family owned six, no, seven houses and they were "camping out" on the 32nd floor of the Carlyle during renovations.

5

At 11:45 a.m., she was hailing a cab. "It's Monday. Which means no trucks or deliveries" she said, leaning forward to give the driver directions. "It should be an easy drive, Ali." Charlotte prided herself on calling drivers by their first, or was it their last names? She wasn't quite sure. But it didn't hurt to be friendly, especially these days. "So just go straight up the West Side Highway, please, and cross 57th to Madison up to 76th Street."

Staring out at the Hudson, Charlotte realized how fiercely attached she was to these early morning rides along the river. Maybe it was the fact the water was always flowing, that it never stopped moving, that consoled her. As she sat back, she let her thoughts meander. Philip had been more obnoxious than usual at the museum benefit. Pawing her thigh, for God's sake. Then there was Pavel, due in from Moscow for his monthly family visit the week after next. She liked Pavel. Maybe too much. Resting her head on the back of the seat, she suddenly felt deliciously drowsy.

The trill of her cell phone woke her from her catnap. Christ. Why had she said hello before checking her caller ID? It was Rita, her most demanding client. She was up in Martha's Vineyard, shutting her house down for the winter.

"Sorry, Rita. But you say you're furious about my $100 surcharge for cleaning the curtains?" Charlotte asked, testily.

"Yes, Charlotte," Rita's voice was unbearably shrill. Adenoidal. "That's correct."

"But you also want to talk about moving the swimming pool ten feet to the right?"

"Correct again, Charlotte. It's ruining our view of the ocean."

"It's flat, Rita. The pool is flat. How is it interfering with your view?" Tapping her fingernails against the seat,

Charlotte worked to keep her temper in check. She couldn't afford to lose this client.

"And the curtains are Japanese Shibori silk," she added. "Hand tie-dyed and shot with platinum. I had to take them to Maurice myself and explain how to launder them. As for the pool... You don't just move a pool ten feet."

"Why not, Charlotte? The Johnsons did. We were over there for drinks on Saturday night."

"And did the Johnsons share with you what the cost of moving their pool might have been?"

"We don't care about the cost," Rita said. Charlotte silently seethed.

"I'll tell you what," Charlotte said in an effort to distract her client while also fantasizing about seeing her liposuctioned, bloated body, floating belly up from the bottom of her cobalt blue pool. "Didn't you say you're flying down with Abe next week?"

"Yes, Charlotte. I did. But I'd like the jet to bring you up here this afternoon. We need to talk."

"Rita, I'd be delighted to talk. I'd also be delighted to cancel the surcharge on the curtains. But I can't possibly get away today."

Mollified by the easy win over her $100, Rita settled for Charlotte's offer to get together the following weekend at her apartment on Fifth.

Charlotte nearly spat when she ended the call.

Haggling over 100 bucks when they'd just spent $300,000 to put in the infinity pool and another $50,000 for the 40-foot gunite "puggle pool" with its own wavelet machine. What the freakin' hell kind of a dog was a puggle, anyway?

No wonder I have such agonizing cramps and can't sleep at night, she thought. Everybody needed more. No one had enough. The whole world was crying poor, *especially* billionaires like Rita, who whined about $100 surcharges for laundering their $55,000 living room curtains. *And what the hell was taking this driver so long*, she groaned, as the cab screeched to a stop.

"We are here, *madam*," Ali said with a smirk.

Charlotte ignored the insult. *No way I look old enough to be a "madam."*

"Go ahead and keep the change," she replied. Charlotte prided herself on being a very good tipper.

Running against the light, she crossed 76th Street and approached the restaurant. Before giving the door a small tug, she smiled graciously at the only "papp" polite enough to snap her photo. The rest of the posse was lounging idly nearby. Charlotte knew that most of the ladies who lunched here came to be seen. As if being seen somehow confirmed that they actually existed. *This is why they also craved the blinding light of the paparazzi's flash*, she thought. For one brief incandescent moment, the light seemed to bring them back to life. Being recognized gave them an illusion of identity.

As Charlotte walked into the narrow crypt-like foyer, she inhaled. "Repressed casual" is how she summed up the Upper East Side uniform of starched jeans and stuffed shirts at this hilariously overpriced bistro. And she'd never liked the room: the low ceilings, all the mauves, the tables too close together. It was as cramped and stiff as the people dining in it.

Anna was standing up and waving as Charles led her to their banquette.

"Ciao! Cara!" she said, kissing her on both cheeks. "What a fabulous suit."

Charlotte was wearing one of her men's Armani pinstripes. She'd had ten of them tailored to fit her lanky 5' 9" build years ago.

"Thanks," she said to Anna, turning quickly to Charles. "I'll have a kir royale, please, the Caesar, and a pesto brushed tilapia."

"Make that two, if you would," Anna chimed in.

"Good choice, ladies," Charles replied, snapping his fingers at a passing busboy. "The tilapia is particularly nice today."

Settling in, Charlotte gave Anna a big smile and glanced around the room.

"Well, there's one group that must have come in through the kitchen," she muttered while nodding towards three women who had obviously just come out from the plastic surgeon's office. With their faces covered in bandages, they looked more like they'd just been air-lifted in from Basra. Slurping soup through straws; even their fish entrée was pureed in the blender.

"You know the most revolting thing of all?" Anna asked, smothering a laugh. "They go vomit in the bathroom after."

"I know, Vincenzo told me," Charlotte said, giving a demure wave to the group.

Vincenzo was their favorite waiter. A native of Milan, he'd recently migrated to Da Albertos, a restaurant downtown.

"Tree tousand a week, I am taking 'ome," he'd crowed, the last time they chatted. "And tonight, Alberto was in de kitchen wid a rock de size of de Gibralter."

The rock, of course, was cocaine, not a diamond.

After Charles had returned with her champagne, Charlotte unfolded her napkin and looked at her friend expectantly. "Okay, Anna. This story about Caroline better be good."

"This, my dear, is better than good," Anna replied, sliding in closer and lowering her voice.

"You know you missed the Armory show Saturday night." The Armory show was New York's most prestigious, carefully-vetted antique show.

"I told you. I had to go to the museum."

"Oh right. Well... You are not going to believe this: The City Sheriff actually came in and confiscated all of Caroline's merchandise."

"No way!!" Charlotte croaked. The scratchy edge of a crouton had caught in her throat.

For years, Caroline had been the mistress of one of the richest old aristos in England. She was so wealthy, she drove her clients around in a 1932 Rolls Royce woodie. (The license plates read "DEKR8.")

"It seems she forgot to pay her plumbing bills. For that new maisonette on Sutton Place. 'Forgot,' as in, for the past *eighteen* months."

My God! The humiliation. The trade will crucify her, Charlotte snickered to herself. "Was she there?" she asked, stabbing at her last crouton.

"No, she left her poor daughter at the booth," Anna said.

"The unholy cruelty of mothers," Charlotte hissed, pushing her plate away as if signaling a need to change the subject.

For once, Anna refused to take the hint. "Aren't you tired of being haunted by your mother, Charlotte?"

"You mean hunted not haunted, Anna. She isn't dead, you know."

"You have to learn what to ask for from people, cara. Asking for what they can't give gets you nowhere."

"I ask for nothing," Charlotte replied, dabbing the linen napkin over her mouth. "That way I'm not disappointed."

Smoothing her platinum silver hair back from her face, Anna swished the champagne around in the bottom of her glass. "It's funny," she said, closing her eyes. "We Italians call orgasm, the little death. Il piccolo morte. But it isn't orgasm, it's disappointment that is the real little death, isn't it?"

Who the hell had taught Anna these things, anyway? Charlotte wondered. "I guess you're right," she said, craning her neck towards the entrance of the restaurant as Charles rushed towards the door and pecked the cheeks of two extremely well-kept blondes. "Every disappointment kills a little bit more of you."

"Oh my God!" Anna whispered. "Look who's here!"

"I know, I know," Charlotte said grinning. "I thought she was in Rio!"

It was Suzie Katz, three times married, three times divorced, making her first public appearance with Gemitila, her new live-in lover and wellness counselor.

"Have you heard they're following that crackpot nutritionist?" Charlotte added. "The one who practices breatharianism?"

Anna leaned in closer. "The guy drinks his own urine, Charlotte. I'm not kidding."

"Well, I certainly hope that's Chardonnay," Charlotte whispered as they watched the blondes touch glasses.

Nibbling her tilapia while the imperious Gemitila summoned Charles with a crook of her index finger, Charlotte shook her head. Whisking their basket of bread off the table, he backed away, bowing. The display of subservience was totally wasted, of course. Gemitila was lost in Suzie's enraptured gaze. *What was it that made these women so merciless to everyone but their dogs?* Charlotte wondered.

"Penny for your thoughts, Charlotte?" Anna was buttoning up her brown cashmere cardigan. "Senti, I don't want you to feel cornered. But surely, there must be something you owe your mother; something you are grateful for?"

Charlotte didn't like answering questions about her mother. Not even when those questions came from Anna. Squirming in the banquette, she fiddled with her spoon. "She taught me how to create and maintain a beautiful façade, Anna."

"Well, she must have been very good at it, cara. Because nobody in this town is as brilliant as you are at creating beautiful façades."

"She was a climber. A phony. Kids at school used to ask me why there were no photos in our house. No grandparents, aunts, uncles, cousins. My mother didn't want them around as witnesses while she climbed the ladder, that's why. So I'd tell them my family was dead."

Anna patted her hand. "Like I said, learn what to ask for, Charlotte. You'll be much happier. And this is my treat," she added, quickly placing her Amex card into the leather folder. "Now I'm going to the ladies room. I want to take a closer look at Gemitila."

It's true, she thought as Anna stopped to speak briefly

with Suzie Katz. *I am grateful for "the eye" that I've inherited from my mother.* Even her father's wealthiest clients (he was an old-fashioned investment banker) had admired what Charlotte's mother had done with their apartment on Fifth and the house out in hoity-toity Alpine, New Jersey. "She has impeccable instincts, dear," Bunny Williams, the doyenne of high-class décor, had once said to Charlotte. The implication being, of course, that Charlotte's mother *had* to rely on instincts. She was shanty Irish. And her husband, Charlotte's father, was a Jew. Not that anyone ever mentioned it. He dressed like the Duke of Windsor.

All that was left now was the place in Alpine. Her father had blown his entire pension, investing in some tax shelter in the Connecticut woods. Two months after he had found out that it was a scam, he'd died of a stroke. He was sixty-two years old. Her mother had only managed to save the house. Furnished with big comfortable canvas-striped couches, threadbare Orientals from old auctions at Parke Bernet and a few 18th century English pieces, Charlotte still liked the feel of it. It was comfortable. And there was nothing contrived or forced about it. Nothing but the people who'd lived in it, she thought.

"Ecco! Are you ready, cara?"

"Definitely. I'm due at Darryl's in twenty minutes."

6

"I've got to have that goddamn belt, do you hear me?" Until Charlotte noticed the Bluetooth blinking in Darryl's ear, it looked like her client was bellowing into thin air. She was also wearing a neck brace. "Listen, it was made for tomorrow night's dress. And I don't care if it's in the house in L.A. or fucking London, you better find it!" Using a circular motion with her finger to indicate to Charlotte that she was just "wrapping up," she dry swallowed a fistful of meds with her other hand and kept right on talking.

"Bundle of nerves" didn't even begin to describe the tension that propelled this tiny, taut woman back and forth across the foyer. Darryl reminded Charlotte of that "Bodies" exhibition that she'd seen downtown. Chinese corpses that had been stripped of flesh to expose the network of nerves that pulsed beneath the skin.

Her 23-million-dollar apartment, one of the last in the 1920s Candela building to be sold intact, had been gutted to the core. The contractor was getting $40,000 a month to "supervise" the job and the super was getting another $4,000 a month to "facilitate" the process. Darryl's husband, a venture capitalist, had also placed a million in escrow to cover the co-op's $4,000-a-day penalty fee for delays. (With the project running four months late, Charlotte estimated that the co-op was already half a million dollars richer.) Darryl's greatest coup, however, had been the purchase of an $801,000 storage closet in the basement.

"It's the last one left, Charlotte," she'd tittered, giddily, on the phone. "And I just can't believe we got it!" Charlotte couldn't believe it, either. But hers was not to reason why a family of three with a 12,000 square-foot apartment, seven other houses, and a giga-yacht needed an $801,000 storage closet!

In the meantime, everything upstairs had been ripped out: the old parquet de Versailles floors, the doors, the fixtures in the bathrooms, kitchen, and pantry, the fireplaces, the Sub-Zero appliances. Even the walls had been stripped of their terracotta and plaster. Charlotte sighed as she circled around the shrouded marble staircase. It had taken two weeks to encapsulate the handrail, the posts, the stringers, and the treads in wiggleboard: a plywood that bent into cylinders. She'd seen this so many times before. Women who threw themselves into the frenzy of renovation, as if by tearing down walls, replacing every inch of wiring and plumbing, hiring fancy French painters, and buying millions of dollars' worth of furniture, they might, somehow, also reinvent themselves. Instead, when the house was finally finished, they often found that they had been gutted to the core themselves—deserted by husbands and on the brink of divorce, with their new showplace homes discreetly placed on the market.

Maybe this explained why Darryl and all of her clients lived in a state of perpetual panic. They were afraid of losing it all. The problem, Charlotte decided as she wandered away from Darryl's voice and down the hall, was perspective. They were as panicked at the prospect of missing a comb-out or gaining an extra two pounds as they were of losing their youth, their husbands, and their money. Yet despite the panic, Charlotte was always impressed by their appearance. Like Darryl (who was now barreling towards her like a woman possessed), it was perfection itself. Every strand of artfully tousled blond hair in place, muscles nicely toned, not even a wrinkle in a linen suit on a summer day.

Gesticulating with one hand, while talking and massaging her shoulder with the other, Darryl signaled for Charlotte to approach. Stepping carefully over floorboards and buckets, her client gave her a kiss. "God almighty!" she said. "My neck!"

"A little tense, huh?" Charlotte said.

"It's not just that. There was a lot of turbulence coming into Teterboro last night."

"Ahhh!" Charlotte replied. "Sorry to hear that!" Darryl was suffering from what she and other clients had dubbed P.J.N.S., *Private Jet Neck Syndrome.* Some of the seats on private jets faced the wrong way for take-offs and landings. Occasionally, the whiplash was so bad, it pinched their nerves.

"So what do you think?" Darryl said, opening her arms as if to embrace the possibilities that surrounded them. They were standing in a library that had been paneled in 19th century French boiserie. "It's going to be gorgeous!" Charlotte replied. "I hope you like my idea of the Louis XV envelope and the polished concrete floors. But I'm not sure about your request for those prison toilets," she added, hesitantly.

"Well, they'll be easy for the help to clean," Darryl said. "And I love the look of cantilevered, stainless steel."

"Good. Then I'll check into it," Charlotte replied, as

docile as a kitten. "But the flush is louder than a 747, Darryl." Her palms were sweating and there was a dull throbbing on the right side of her abdomen. As her client pivoted to the right, Charlotte imagined planting a poker in the back of her head.

Darryl still hadn't stopped talking. "It's not like I'm doing the whole house with prison toilets, Charlotte. It's just the library, the master suite and Tim's room."

Tim was the couple's seven-year-old son. "And by the way, for Tim, I'm thinking something along the lines of a *dojo*, you know? He loves karate. His *sensei* told me about this old Japanese guy who comes in and hand weaves grass mats, just like in a real tatami room."

"Right," Charlotte said. "A dojo, why not?"

"Now, Charlotte. How are you doing on those photographs for the Carlyle?"

"I brought them with me," she replied. "They're out in the front hall."

"Oh! I'm soooo relieved, Charlotte. I want something so hip, it hurts."

As Charlotte untied the string around her package, Darryl's Bluetooth blinked.

"Oh My God! Oh My God!" she squealed, wrenching it out, when the three-foot portraits were revealed. "I adore them!"

The workers had huddled around and were staring, goggle-eyed, at the photographs.

"The German artist calls them 'Delirium,'" Charlotte explained, laying out the series of six black and white nude couples. "They were shot exactly three minutes after orgasm."

"Well, I cannot *wait* to get them back to the hotel, Charlotte. They're divine!"

"I knew you'd like them," Charlotte said, peeking at her watch. "But listen. I'm headed downtown. I have to talk to the architects about visas for your French painters and the Italian mosaic team."

"Oh, I am just *so thrilled*, Charlotte. We're going to make this an absolute dream house."

Picking up her bag, Charlotte kissed Darryl goodbye and hitched a ride down to the basement in the freight elevator. The visit had left her feeling utterly deflated.

7

Charlotte collapsed on her down-filled couch. *Prison toilets… Christ!* She thought. What an atrocious waste of a day. No new prospects on Craigslist. No Murano glass for Pavel. And she'd forgotten her cell at Boulud. Charlotte pushed the play button on her answering machine.

"Please, please, Charlotte. Say you'll come!" It was Vicky. "I'm so stressed out, I'm flying Tom down on the jet. You could come together. Call me." Tom was an occasional friend of Charlotte's and one of the best masseurs in town.

"Nobody has hands like him," Vicky had extolled rapturously, after Charlotte had sent him to the house as a gift.

The thing is, Tom was as good at massaging certain truths as he was knotted muscles. For instance, he was gay. Like totally gay. But somehow, Vicky still didn't know.

"I have these fantasies," she'd said over a long lunch at

the oh-so-staid but reliable San Domenico. "I can't help it, Charlotte. I mean, the man is so empathic..."

It was almost funny, that the most selfish people on the planet did nothing but talk about empathy. No way she was flying out to Aspen.

The next message was from her mother. "Hi, dear. You haven't returned any of my calls, not even on your cell. I'm worried. Are you all right?" *Worried?* That would be a first.

The last message was from Dr. Greene. "Hello, Charlotte. It's 5:15. I haven't heard from you. I know that we've discussed ending your therapy. But this will be the second session you've missed. I will have to charge you."

Perfect, Charlotte muttered to herself. *Another $450 down the Toto toilet.* She was already two months late on her Amex bill. Better to be two months late with her period. Being pregnant would be a joy compared to being cut off by Amex in New York City. What was it that old advertising C.E.O had said to her years ago?

"You're a member of what we call 'the experiential generation,' dear."

"Meaning what?" Charlotte had asked.

"Meaning you spend all your money now and save nothing for later," he'd chuckled. "Now how 'bout experiencing a nice glass of $350 Germain-Robin brandy?"

Kicking off her flats and hoisting herself up from the couch, she walked down the narrow hall towards her bedroom. The pink silk sari walls looked as fresh as the day she'd tacked them up. While her clients insisted on spending fortunes and buying only from top notch textile dealers, Charlotte preferred to hunt for saris in the tacky Mom and

Pop stores on Lexington Avenue. She loved the strings of garish colored blinking lights strung up inside the windows, the pungent restaurant smells of oily curries and spices, and the cheerful rat-tat-tat of Urdu, the language of Pakistani taxi drivers. Picnicking from the hoods of their cars, the drivers would stand around and gossip as Charlotte sat in one of the shops, drinking tea and haggling as if her life depended on it.

Sometimes, like with the sari on her hallway walls, she'd get lucky. The owner would pat her hand and ask her to wait as he wandered off into a dimly lit backroom. Charlotte would drink her tea and fantasize about discovering some long lost treasure like the Baroda carpet. Seven feet long, the rug was a piece of soft deerskin studded with a million pearls, over 2,000 rose-cut diamonds, and hundreds of rubies and emeralds. It had disappeared in the 1940s during Partition when an Indian maharani had sent it to Switzerland for "safekeeping."

The sari on her walls may not have been quite as precious as the Baroda carpet. But when the dealer emerged from his backroom, he treated it almost as reverently. Unfolding the yards of heavy silk from a bed of wrinkled white tissue, he'd run his fingers along the hand-embroidered borders. "Real gold filigree, Miss." he'd boasted. "A wedding sari from long ago." Two cups of tea and fifteen minutes of bargaining later, the sari was hers.

Then she remembered that it was Paul who had helped her tack it up. Two years, they'd been together. And he'd dumped her for some twenty-three-year-old British party girl with an I.Q. of 4.

"She's OD'ed on Gs and Es," he reported the night he called from New York Hospital. As in grams of cocaine and ecstasy. Apparently, the girl's father sent some lackey from an international concierge service to pick up his own daughter in the emergency room. There was this girl strung out and nearly dead, and all Paul wanted to talk about was the concierge service.

"It's free, Charlotte. I mean, it's part of the lifestyle management team at her condo."

Charlotte assumed that people used these services for booking front row seats at fashion shows and last minute tables at Nobu. Not for picking up comatose daughters. "Uhhuh," was the only word she'd managed to summon up from the depths of sleep. Did he really think she cared? Who did he think he was, waking her at 2 in the morning to talk about his new girlfriend?

This was the problem with opening yourself up to people; when you were generous and loving and serving, always serving, the needs of others. They turned on you. They exploited you. *My whole life is about other people,* Charlotte sighed. *And I never get any thanks.* Neatly folding back the top sheet on her bed and plumping the goose down pillows, Charlotte tried not to think of the shrunken old lady she'd seen shuffling through the checkout line at D'Agostinos. As Charlotte flipped through the pages of the *Enquirer* and the woman exchanged green points for TV dinners and Bumble Bee tuna fish, Charlotte imagined herself at a similar age, hunched over and hiding the hump on her back with shawls and droopy, oversized clothing.

She could sense the woman's shame, her humiliation.

Years of bending over backwards, of pleasing and appeasing, and this was her reward. But this is what protecting and serving people was all about. Belittling yourself. Making yourself seem insignificant and small. Some people, Charlotte supposed, made themselves small simply to survive and others for the sake of love. That didn't make them any less "dysfunctional," as her shrink would say.

Charlotte's neck stiffened as she pummeled the pillows. Swatting at the blizzard of feathers that tickled her neck and face, she wiped the beads of sweat off her forehead. The pillows looked as if they'd been disemboweled. *Enough. Enough feeling sorry for yourself, Charlotte.* Dragging the dry cleaning into her closet, she wrenched the plastic sheet off a wool jacket and reached for a padded hanger.

Cry me a river, build me a bridge, and get over it! Isn't that what Vicky's daughter had said to her mother the night Vicky complained, yet again, about being so frantically busy and tired?

"Busy doing *what,* Mom?" the girl had asked, eyes flashing with one exquisitely manicured hand on her hip. "Taking care of *yourself*? That's pretty much *all* you do all day, isn't it?"

Charlotte was stunned. Even if it were sort of true, that wasn't the point. With a kid like that, Charlotte herself would also be up and working out at the crack of dawn with a body talk practitioner, a yoga instructor, a Reiki teacher, and a guy who rolled hot rocks across her back. In fact, she'd probably bury the kid in hot rocks.

The phone was ringing. *Let it go*, Charlotte thought. *It's been a long day. Take a bath.* Then it rang again. What if it was Pavel, calling from Moscow? She ran into the bedroom, bumping her shin so hard on the edge of the bed that her eyes watered as she picked up.

"Hey! Charlotte, darling. It's me."

"Hi, Vicky. I got your message but..."

"Forget the message, Charlotte. I spoke to my daughter this afternoon, and I'm worried sick."

"Vicky, you're always worried sick about Rose." Rubbing her bruised shin, she sat down on her bed. If only she hadn't picked up ... Vicky's calls went on *forever*.

"She was caught shoplifting at Bergdorf's, okay?"

"Jesus," Charlotte whispered. The kid had just returned from some chaperone-escorted, Shop-Till-You-Drop tweenie tour of Paris. What the hell was she doing shoplifting?

"So what'd she steal?" Charlotte asked, innocently.

"Two 80-dollar books on Buddhism," Vicky replied. "From the Home department on 7."

Charlotte rolled her eyes. "My God! At least, she has a sense of humor, Vicky. I mean, c'mon! *Stealing* books on Buddhism?"

"It's not funny, Charlotte. She told me they were a thank-you gift for Paris."

"Well, I guess it's the thought that counts," Charlotte said, picking up a pair of clippers from inside her bedside table drawer and clipping a hang nail on her pinkie.

"You don't have children, Charlotte. You can't imagine how disturbing all this is."

Charlotte took a deep breath and exhaled. What if Amex really did cut her off? Maybe she could borrow the eight grand from Vicky. The two of them never talked about money, of course. It wasn't that the rich didn't enjoy talking about money. They did. They talked about it all the time. But only amongst themselves.

"The thing is," Vicky was saying. "I'd really like to talk to my daughter, that's all. Not just about the shoplifting. She's not eating, either. The other night, she was talking about how cool it was to be 'ano.'"

"Ano?" Charlotte queried.

"Anorexic. They abbreviate everything."

"'JK, Mom, JK,' she said after. Just kidding. But honestly, Charlotte. I don't know what to do. We can't seem to communicate. She tunes me right out."

Charlotte laughed out loud. "What planet are you living on, Vicky? Nobody her age communicates, anymore. Not face-to-face."

Moving into the bathroom, she squeezed her tooth-whitening gel on her mouth plate, still cradling the phone next to her ear as Vicky chattered on. It was faster and easier to plug into iPods, log onto Facebook, or IM or blog and compulsively text while chatting on cell phones. The whole experience of communicating had become, *literally*, disembodied. But Charlotte was a visual person, so it didn't bother her that in moving into this new dimension, language had lost the power of nuance, of gesture. "Wrds" were words no matter how you spelled them. And without this new technology, there'd be no community out there like Craigslist. *My other life*, she thought, reminding herself to visit Kinko's first thing in the morning.

"Charlotte, you're not listening," Vicky said. "I know you're not listening."

"Sorry. I'm distracted. And I've got to go," Charlotte replied." I have a crazy day tomorrow with a new client. I'm exhausted."

"I wanted you to come down here with Tom. You promised, Charlotte. I need you."

Charlotte hadn't promised. They hadn't even talked about it. But she hesitated. Aspen might be a good place to ask for the money. On second thought, she had too much to do. "I can't, Vicky. And you're back the day after tomorrow, anyway. We'll talk then."

"Fine," Vicky said petulantly. "There's someone on the other line. I'm hanging up."

Finishing up her treatment in the bathroom, Charlotte recalled a scene outside Vicky's building. It was right before the kid's trip to Paris. As the doorman hailed her a cab, one of Vicky's drivers pulled up to the curb in the daughter's "school car." It was a red Mercedes station wagon with her name, ROSE1, on the license plates. The kid, who stepped out of the car, dragging her $750 Bisonte knapsack, weighed about 90 pounds. *Now here was a true crime*, thought Charlotte as she slipped into her La Perla silk pyjamas. (A Christmas gift from Anna.) The child was so thin, she was almost transparent. But still her mother couldn't see. Twenty pounds lighter than she'd been in college, she couldn't see herself in this wasted, half-starved, unsexed child.

8

She liked the privacy of the booths at Kinko's. This particular branch at 12th Street between University and Fifth was a favorite. Even with the nearby university, it was quiet. The walls of her booth were scribbled with graffiti. "jason loves jenny!" "FUCK PHYSICS!" She'd been commuting between Furniture and Collectibles since 8 a.m. Chewing on a bit of blueberry muffin, she focused on her screen. The Furniture category had been a total waste of time. A blur of postings for TV armoires, entertainment centers, mattresses, storage platforms, more mattresses and recliners. *God! How America's sedentary minds love recliners*, Charlotte thought.

Her scroll through Collectibles had been even more disappointing. If you are what you collect, Charlotte pondered, what would future anthropologists conclude about a culture that seemed to collect nothing but baseball cards, comics, Elvis Christmas ornaments, Barbie batgirls on motorcycles and Beanie Babies? And what the fuck was a Talking Furby doll? Is this what archeologists would dig up and study a thousand years from now as they sifted through the ashes of what had been known as the greatest city in the world? She stopped and clicked. "A first edition Torah-1962. $150." *Huh?* Oh, and the Dracula Style Black Coffin for $36. "Never been outta our basemant." That was a good one, too.

Giving her aching eyes a rest, she blocked out the twinge of a cramp. Anna had finally convinced her to make an appointment with her gynecologist for an ultrasound. She was due at the Diagnostic Labs on 21st and 2nd Avenue at 2 o'clock. Charlotte hated the idea of anyone looking inside her. But the pain had become more frequent and intense since her afternoon with the "Model Homemaker." Taking another bite from her blueberry muffin, she washed it down with some orange juice and wondered why there hadn't been any follow-up in the news after her last murder. Not even in the *Post*. Surely, the police had identified a pattern. Both victims were female, rich and lived on the Upper East Side.

This was the beauty, of course, of choosing her "victims" from Craigslist. In cyberspace, she was a phantom. Just another sexless, anonymous shopper. Tracking her down in the real world would take physical evidence. And Charlotte was certain that she'd left no trace of that. Still ... the silence was unsettling.

Bingo! Charlotte almost knocked over her cup of coffee.

"Three piece, custom-made Vuitton luggage set. $3,000. No best offers. Price firm. Please e-mail."

She clicked and checked out the photo. The minute she saw the details about location, 'UES, Obviously,' she e-mailed back for an appointment. *Obviously?*

This was the kind of arrogance that came with the territory inhabited by her "victims." The Upper East Side, her kill zone. The richest, greediest 1.8 square miles in the United States.

Other people might think of a world gone to hell in terms of famine in faraway Darfur, genocide in Rwanda, the slums of Mumbai and Manila. Not Charlotte. For her, that world gone to hell stretched from Bergdorf's on 57th Street and Fifth, north to 96th Street, across Madison to Park. It was a world that mistook trend for truth, fame for faith, and money (when it applied to marriage) for meaning. It was the land of the professional time-killer where a woman's only job in life was to amuse herself to death. Oh yeah. And to redecorate.

In targeting this tiny area with its 70-million-dollar penthouses and 50-million-dollar townhouses, some might say that Charlotte was biting the hand that fed her. What did they know about the hands that rarely offered her anything more than a glass of still Badoit water? All they ever saw were photos of smiling faces at parties in the Styles Section of the *New York Times*. Charlotte knew better. Like all those who served the voracious needs of money's mistresses: building supers, doormen, life coaches, pet psychics, nutritionists, waiters, chauffeurs, housekeepers, nannies, concierges, personal assistants and trainers, Charlotte knew all about the panic and the rage that seethed beneath the glittering surface She dealt with it every day.

Even if she understood it—the loneliness, the frustration in dealing with such tyrannical husbands—there was something about the fury that roiled beneath the façade of such grotesquely over-privileged lives that Charlotte found loathsome. That poverty of the spirit—the purposelessness. It was a kind of moral anarchy. Once upon a time, Charlotte imagined that anger might have triggered social change, even revolution. Now all the rage had turned inward. Women like Vicky, Darryl and Rita preferred to talk about moving their swimming pools or about the weather. (The weather, in fact, had become such a hot topic that Charlotte had sat next to the world's most famous fog expert at Vicky's last dinner. After twenty minutes of listening to details about harnessing water content, electrostatic precipitation, and acid rain, she'd wanted to pull her hair out).

"God is the definition of home." The line, from an Emily Dickinson poem that Charlotte had read in college, was taped across the top of her office "dream board," a collage of drawings, photos, swatches and other inspirational fragments. This call-to-action had given birth to her career ambitions. Ambitions that been whittled away and corrupted by her need to submit to her clients' whims; to compromise and to constantly coddle and cajole. Charlotte was doing the devil's work now, because nobody actually *lived* in the houses that she spent such obscene sums of money and time decorating. They were designed solely to inspire envy, monstrous amounts of envy. The sterility within these camera-ready homes reflected little more than impotence—the same impotence that prompted the poor to kill.

So Charlotte was cleaning house, so to speak. She was purging herself of that same amorphous, soul-shriveling rage. She was delivering a message, making a point. Greed wasn't good. And marrying money wasn't a shortcut. It was a dead end.

9

She'd arrived at the doctor's office at exactly 1:45. Anna had begged to keep her company, but Charlotte had turned her down. Asking for comfort was a great deal more difficult for her than giving it. After filling out insurance forms and passing over her $20 co-pay, she'd been waiting for more than an hour in a dirty, beige lobby. No one had even had the courtesy to apologize or explain the reason for the delay.

Why were these rooms always so drab and depressing? She asked herself. How much did it cost to water a plant? To slap a fresh coat of paint on the walls? To smile? The sharp nosed, thin-lipped receptionist had barely grunted when Charlotte finally lost her patience and insisted on paging the technician.

When the woman leapt out from behind the lab door, scowling, Charlotte stepped back as if she'd been ambushed.

"Follow me," the woman barked, as she headed down a long, dark corridor. Opening the door to a small cubicle, she ordered Charlotte to remove all her clothes and put on a paper robe. "Leave the front open," she added, before slamming the door behind her. Charlotte was shivering as she lay in the dark on an examining table with her knees up. She didn't dare move for fear of ripping the thin sheet of tissue that lay stretched beneath her.

The excruciating pains had started in college. It was Vicky who had taken her to the local emergency room and explained the symptoms to an intern. After two days of tests and no sleep, the pain had finally subsided.

"There's nothing *physically* wrong with you," the inept young doctor had told her.

"Nothing we can find, anyway. But I'd like to recommend the name of a good psychiatrist."

Charlotte had tightened the belt of her robe, repressing a flash of anger. It wasn't just the careless arrogance of the doctors. It was the unforgivable fact that her mother hadn't even bothered to make an appearance at her bedside.

She was down in New Orleans, celebrating some honorary degree that Tulane had given her father. As if he needed another honorary degree. Years later, when Dr. Greene had the gall to suggest that it might be her own rage, twisting up her insides and eating through her stomach lining, Charlotte had wanted to kill him.

A thin shaft of light pierced through the gloom as the technician re-entered the room. Squeezing a jelly lubricant all over the wand-like probe, she then placed a pillow under Charlotte's hips. Charlotte had never felt so exposed, so out of control. As the cold, plastic probe delved deeper and deeper inside her, her helplessness triggered a spurt of pure terror.

"Stay still!" the woman hissed. "Or we'll be here all night."

For forty interminable minutes, she was subjected to the technician's ruthless intrusions; to the clicking and stopping, clicking and stopping, as she photographed the shadowy depths of her womb.

Charlotte knew there was something in there. She sensed it. It was something ugly and vile. Made of her own hair and muscle, of bits of bone, blood and the tears she had never shed, it clung to her and grew, sapping her energy and sucking the air she breathed. Nothing could expel it. It had always hurt, this thing that grew inside her. It hurt so much that she imagined it was tearing her insides apart. When she smiled and politely asked the technician what she was seeing on the screen, the woman ignored her. It was only when Charlotte closed her legs and threatened to leave that she responded.

"I'm not allowed to answer your questions, ma'am. It's company policy."

"So when I will know the results?" Charlotte asked as the woman wiped the wand clean with a white towel.

"We send them to your doctor," the woman replied coldly, handing her a wad of Kleenex. "But I wouldn't worry about it *too* much," she added casually. "Now please wait until I check the film."

"What the hell did that mean?" Charlotte whispered to herself. "I wouldn't worry *too* much?" Wiping the lubricant off her belly, she imagined the woman casually gossiping about her cancer with colleagues. When the technician stuck her head in the door and told her she could go, Charlotte struggled like a zombie through the motions of putting on her clothes and trembled. *What if it is a tumor?* she thought. *How will I pay for it all? How will I work?*

10

She was walking so fast towards the News Bar on 3rd Avenue and 23rd Street, she was short of breath. There had been something horrifyingly familiar about the experience of lying on that table; about the helplessness. Slowing down her pace as the first cramp snaked through her gut and the crowd jostled past her, a memory sprang up like a clown coiled up in a jack-in-the-box.

The family was in Barbados and her mother had offered her a swimming lesson. She was six. She could feel the burning sand beneath her toes as they ambled towards the promise of a cool blue sea. They were together so rarely that even though the sand burned, Charlotte refused to rush.

When the pebbles on the shore cut into the soft soles of her feet and the waves loomed larger, she held more tightly to her mother's hand and smiled.

"Just try and relax," her mother had said, as she held Charlotte firmly beneath her small arms and together they bobbed on the crest of the waves. Charlotte wanted so much to give something to her mother; something that would make her proud.

It was just at the moment when her limbs began to unlock and she felt so light, so buoyant, she laughed out loud, that her mother let her go. And down she went, caught in the steel-like grip of cold, blue water. It had puzzled her, the strength of that watery grip, before the panic took hold and she opened her mouth to cry out. Later, on the beach, her throat stinging from retching up sea and sand, her mother had hugged her. "I told you to relax, dear," she'd said with a grin. "That's how you learn to float." Charlotte had never put her head beneath the surface of the sea again.

Punching at the glass door as if to punch the memory back into its box, Charlotte entered the News Bar. After handing over her credit card to the cashier, she looked for a seat. Every computer was open. Heading towards the back of the room, she sat down, typed in the password for her latest hotmail account, and scrolled through endless junk mail. Yes! There it was. A message from 12ft.candy@gm.com:

Subj: Vuitton Luggage
Date: 10/3/2009
To: CoreenG.@hotmail.com
Dear Coreen:

The luggage was custom-made at Vuitton in Paris. My price is firm. If you'd like to come by and take a look, I'll be here Friday at 4. I'm at 32 E. 65th St. Why don't you call me? cell: #917-655-7542
Best, Amy

Charlotte felt just the tiniest clutch of hope tug at her heart. Noting down the number before deleting the message, she exited and rebooted. She'd follow up with Amy from a payphone later.

11

"Cavolfiore, Charlotte. My mother told me I was born in a cauliflower. Can you imagine this?" Anna was sliding off the red upholstered barstool when Charlotte's hand shot out and propped her up by the elbow. "I never forgive myself for leaving them, do you know that? I still send money home."

Charlotte took a slow sip of her glacially iced martini. They'd been the first to arrive three hours ago at the Temple Bar on Lafayette Street. And Anna had been talking ever since. Charlotte sat as still as a statue, afraid that the slightest movement might destroy the magic of the moment.

"I still have this little box on my night table," Anna added, running her finger along the rim of her glass. "When I am depressed, I open that drawer and pick up the 500 lira piece that I landed with in New York. Fifty cents. It was all I had when my plane touched down, Charlotte."

Removing her hand from Anna's elbow, Charlotte

nibbled a salted cashew. "Everyone thinks you've made millions, Anna. After so many years and so many famous clients."

Anna choked and grinned. "I have nothing, Charlotte. Nothing. For twenty-five years, I have this golden angel on my shoulder. I think it is like this for everyone. There is a time in life when an angel looks over you. And then it is gone. But I am not jealous. Last week, I was visiting an old client in his apartment. Beauty was everywhere. On this one table, there was fifteen million dollars' worth of priceless objects. Just one in your pocket and you would never have to work again."

Charlotte grimaced. "How can you stand it, Anna? My clients don't even know what they have. It infuriates me."

Anna turned on her stool and caressed Charlotte's cheek. "So what, cara? It is the memories I live on. Twelve years ago, I was the guest of an English lord. He had a passport like an accordion and treated us all to a trip on the Queen Elizabeth. Every night, we are with the Captain." Taking a last sip of her third martini, Anna sighed. "And the parties in Capri? They were the loveliest in the world in the '70s. And my trips to Nassau with my Texan client? Always in a private jet with such generous gifts. No, I have been lucky, Charlotte. So much luckier than my unhappy clients."

Charlotte slid a fifty under her glass. "I wish I could see it that way, Anna. I really do. But my clients aren't half as generous or interesting as yours." Cajoling Anna off her stool, she pointed towards the door. "And now it's time for bed, my friend. For both of us."

Picking her way through the group of raucous smokers

who stood on the sidewalk outside, Charlotte hailed a cab. Opening the door, she protected Anna's head with her hand and guided her, gently, into the backseat. "We'll talk tomorrow," she said.

"Si cara, domani!" Anna replied with a stiff little wave of her wrist as Charlotte turned and began to walk briskly home. She'd had three martinis with Anna. Two was her usual limit. But sometimes she had to bend the rules. The cold, harsh air slowly sobered her up. She even stopped on Grand Street and raised her eyes towards the full moon. Like most New Yorkers, Charlotte never looked up. She focused on what was ahead or beneath her.

All great bars cast a spell, she thought, searching vaguely for a star. And it wasn't just the alcohol. At the Temple, it was the comfort of darkness, the satiny gleam of polished woods, the glitter of glass bottles lined up like little soldiers against the bar. *It was the illusion of order*, she decided. That and the captivatingly odd but seductive combination of intimacy and anonymity. This is what had almost bewitched Charlotte into telling Anna about her missions.

The minute she walked into her apartment, she rushed over to her answering machine. No blinking red light. *What did it mean if the doctor hadn't called?* Was he still waiting for results from the lab? Part of her wasn't sure that she wanted to know what had been found on the sonogram. She'd lived with the pain this long, she figured, and it hadn't killed her. But she had no appetite, no energy. All she wanted to do was to crawl into bed and sleep.

Hauling herself towards the bedroom, she grabbed a washcloth from the bathroom, soaked it in ice-cold water, and climbed in between the fresh, cool sheets. Worrying was useless. She'd have to think about something else. She'd think about Pavel.

Anna had seated her next to him at one of her dinners at home. "I'm not matchmaking, cara. I just know you'll like him."

Her friend was right. The two of them had talked non-stop, right through dessert. Charlotte liked everything about Pavel. He was stunning: tall and all muscle, the only man who had ever picked her straight up off the ground when he hugged her goodbye. Charlotte was not accustomed to being hugged. With a head of disheveled white hair and eyes as blue as anti-freeze, he wore a dark wool Brioni suit that fit so impeccably, it looked as if it had been born on him.

Unlike Paul, Pavel wasn't just a nice piece of arm candy. Charlotte was in awe of the Russian's recklessness, his resilience. The story of his success, or the story he chose to tell her, was full of gaping holes and mystery, of exaggerations that seemed almost as ridiculous as his realities and truths.

According to Pavel, since the Iron Curtain had come down in 1991, he had survived a burning building (his own), a sinking ship (also his own), the threat of being shot down over Uzbekistan, and other disasters too numerous to name. "This is why I have white hair, Charlotte. My white hair is the history of all of Russia since Glasnost." But no one laughed more uproariously at his own disasters than Pavel. And she admired him for that, too. Everything about Pavel, including his physical size, made other people's lives seem puny, insignificant.

"I'm warning you, Charlotte," Anna had said to her later

as they washed up the dishes in her tiny kitchen. "The only people in the world who can deal with Russians in business are Italians."

"Don't be stupid," Charlotte had said with exasperation. "We get along famously."

"Ah! But we Italians understand the virtues of being flexible with the truth. Americans don't."

"I do," said Charlotte with a smile."I know all about being flexible with the truth."

Anxiously eyeing the numbers on her digital clock, Charlotte estimated the number of hours of sleep ahead. She'd tried television and hot milk. Now she was burning her way through James Salter's *A Sport and a Pastime. Like a first-class surgeon pithing a frog,* she thought, mulling over his brilliant dissection of a doomed love affair. It was two o'clock. If she fell asleep by three, she'd only get five hours. Every time Charlotte felt herself dozing off, her heart would race. Her eyes would pop open as wide as a child staring at a shark that brushes itself up against an aquarium window.

When her shrink had suggested that Charlotte's insomnia might be a sign of depression, she'd agreed to try a cycle of antidepressants. But she was weaning herself off them. Charlotte suspected that the five-milligram pills were secretly stripping her of her identity; that the shrink was colluding in this conspiracy and that every time she swallowed a pill, another uniquely precious part of herself vanished.

Repositioning the pillow between her legs, she suddenly thought of the children's room up at Rita's house on the Vineyard; of opening a Dutch red enamel door to a room painted in blue and white stripes, the blue so translucent it seemed to glow from within and the walls of a nursery washed in the palest iridescent pink, a pink that shimmered like the inside of a spiral seashell. It was the optimism, the fearlessness, the certainty of color that astonished Charlotte. And this was precisely how she felt after completing her missions: fearless, astonished, joyous; as if the whole grey, desolate world had been drenched in buckets of pure, radiant color.

12

Rolling her neck to loosen the kinks, Charlotte lingered by the kitchen window and watched a cruise ship slip beneath the Verranzano Bridge. What was the name of that virus? The one that had hundreds of sunburned, drunken honeymooners retching all over the decks afraid to touch each other not to mention everything else from doorknobs to forks. All of these germs and viruses were getting nastier and nastier. *Just like the world they're mutating in*, Charlotte thought, taking a last sip from her cappuccino.

Pulling on her old shearling jacket and pocketing the piece of paper with Amy's cell phone number, Charlotte fumbled around in the hall closet. She was looking for her new Nikes. *How long had it been since the last time,* she wondered. Too long, was the answer.

It was all the schizophrenic struggling. The protecting, the serving, the listening. It was clients like Darryl and Rita, beeping, buzzing around in her head, bitching. And her mother calling. It was her credit card bills and waiting for news from the doctor. How much longer could she postpone the pleasure, the ecstasy that came with release? What if the woman with the Vuitton changed her mind? Tying the laces of her sneakers, Charlotte avoided looking near the fireplace.

Like ex-smokers who keep a single cigarette in plain sight, she was testing her will. Resisting temptation. The poker sat there, all gold and shiny, patiently waiting for the moment when she would finally give in. Closing the door and locking it behind her, Charlotte ran for the elevator.

13

Waiting for a break in the traffic, she crossed West Broadway and dug into her pockets for a quarter. Charlotte was hardly a fool. She knew that rich women were surrounded by more lackeys than most heads of state. They hated being alone. But the precariousness, the element of risk, even the danger of being caught, heightened the anticipation. Occasionally, when a tiny window of opportunity opened up, and Charlotte slipped through it to accomplish her task, she was convinced that she been anointed; that there was something almost holy about her missions. Five minutes later, she hung up the payphone and smiled. She'd left a message, confirming the rendezvous with Amy for the next day.

Feeling a surge of energy course through her veins, she began her speed walk. She was covering sixty, seventy blocks a day now. She had the pacing down to an art. It wasn't about being the first to cross when the light went green; it was about being the last to slither and squeeze through the threat of solid red. There was no room for the fainthearted or the cautious on these marathons of hers. On a good day, speed-walking was a metaphor for life; a reminder that she knew exactly where she was going and refused to waste a minute getting there.

Much like her relationship with Craigslist, the walking was also a means of reinforcing her connection with the city. Every belch of steam that shot up in the street, every gust of warm air that whooshed up from the grates beneath her feet and caressed her legs, reminded Charlotte that the city was breathing; that it was part of her. Forced to stop briefly at Canal for the rush of traffic coming in from New Jersey through the Holland Tunnel, she laughed out loud.

There'd been a blind item on Page Six of the *Post* this morning: Some network anchorman had been caught screwing his kid's nanny on (what else?) the nanny cam. *How ironic is that?* Charlotte hooted to herself. The guy doesn't even know the system's up and running. And there he is, caught with his pants down by his own wife.

Serves 'em both right, Charlotte giggled. She wondered if this was the same guy her friend Tom worked for. Every night, the guy had a sixty-minute head massage before going on the air.

"For what?" Charlotte had asked Tom, "So he can read better?"

When the light changed, she was already halfway across Canal and marching past the Soho Grand Hotel. Twice a week, Tom also worked on the anchorman's wife and their two teenage kids. The wife, like Vicky, was thinking about becoming a Buddhist. Charlotte had seen photographs of her private mediation room in *New York Magazine*'s Tranquility Issue. It was a vast 1,000-square-foot space with a magnificent view of Central Park, complete with a $40,000 head of Buddha. Charlotte was no expert in Buddhism, but she did know that the religion came into being for people who had nothing. Not the other way around. Did this woman actually aspire to having nothing? No. She wanted it all. Being a Buddhist was just another way of having *more*. Of having peace of mind plus the Jimmy Choos, the Gulfstream, Christmas in Parrot Cay and the ranch in Wyoming.

Deafened by the sound of horns, Charlotte caught a glimpse of a cab driver shaking his fist at her and shrieking. "You crazy! You crazy bitch!" She'd been walking so fast, she'd stepped right into the middle of traffic on 23rd Street. Sweat was trickling down her neck.

Damn! Glancing at her wristwatch, she realized that she was going to be late for the dealer who'd called about the Murano. She'd have to jump on the subway.

Charlotte despised the subway. It wasn't just the fear of being trapped in a tunnel. It was all those *people* crushed up against her. *Touching her*. Charlotte didn't like being touched by strangers. And some of them stank. Spritzing herself with a dose of Caleche ("Every girl needs a signature scent," was one of her mother's style mottos), Charlotte ran down the stairs of the station, bought a single trip Metro Card and hurried through the turnstile. Gingerly pushing her way into a car on the number 6 train, she sat down, closed her eyes and began to hum, softly, to herself.

When Charlotte had been frightened or uncomfortable

as a child, she'd developed this trick of singing. One of her teachers at Chapin had told her that there were these Aborigines in Australia who believed the whole world, everything in it, from stones and lakes to the seas, mountains, and even man, had been literally sung into existence. It was the most romantic thing Charlotte had ever heard. But when she started singing herself to sleep at night—the only thing that helped console her in those tortuous, lonely, sleepless hours after she went to bed—she had been told to stop.

"Shh! Your father's working. Keep quiet, Charlotte," her mother had ordered. "Or I'll punish you."

Insisting that Charlotte eat her dinner with two silver napkin rings clenched between her upper arms and torso was one of her mother's favorite forms of punishment. "It's to help your posture, dear," she'd say. "You'll thank me for your straight back when you're older." What kind of parent punishes their own child for sounding happy or for finding a way of fighting off the demons in the dark? That was the thing, you see? By making noise, Charlotte was telling the demons that she was still awake. Not until later did she discover that some demons don't wait until you're asleep. Some attack and hurt you, even when you're wide awake.

Her phone vibrated just as the train was pulling into the 68th Street station. Taking the stairs two at a time, she raced up Lexington, over to Madison, and flipped open her screen. The doctor had left a voice mail.

"Charlotte. I just got your results. And there's really

nothing to worry about. But I'd like you to schedule an appointment. Please call my secretary and she'll set it up."

Her hands were shaking as she punched in his digits. The word "really"... It sounded like he was minimizing something. It wasn't quite casual enough.

"Good morning. This is Dr. Thorpe's office."

"Hi! I'm Charlotte Wolfe. The doctor..."

"Yes, he spoke to me, Ms. Wolfe. We have a cancellation next Thursday at 11:15. Will that work for you?"

Charlotte gulped. "There's nothing sooner? I'm—"

"Anxious? I'm sure you are, dear. But the doctor's out of town. May I pencil you in?"

"Forget the pencil," Charlotte retorted. "Use a pen. I'll be there."

"Very good, Ms. Wolfe. See you then."

Scanning Madison, she zeroed in on her destination. Lamiere was the name of the shop. "It's supposed to be L*u*miere," the dealer, Ed, had chuckled years ago. "But the painters spelled it wrong."

Considering this guy bought most of his stuff from flea markets and jacked up the price thirty times, you'd think he could afford to repaint one letter.

"Charlotte, how lovely to see you!" Ed shouted as he opened the door. Gracefully sidestepping his hug, she smiled instead. Rumor had it, Ed had been wearing the same pair of greasy black pleather pants and matching beanie for twenty years. He even smelled oily. "You too, Ed. I can't wait to see what you have for me."

"You are going to LOVE it. I didn't even bother to put it out in the shop. That's how sure I am about it."

Leading the way through his labyrinth of lighting, Ed took her to the back. And there, standing all by itself in a corner of the workroom, was the perfect Murano lamp. "See? The emerald is the same color as your eyes, Charlotte. And it's genuine 1920s. Even the base is glass."

"You're right. It's gorgeous," Charlotte said, fondling the five-foot pole of clear emerald, hand-blown glass. The carnival-like stripe of twisted gold inside almost brought tears to her eyes.

"And not a nick on it," Ed announced.

"Now go ahead, Ed. Knock me out. How much?"

"The net, Charlotte? $13,000."

"Oh c'mon, Ed. I've known you a long time. I want the net net."

Ed shrugged his shoulders and sighed. "$11,000. Can't go a penny less. The list is $18,000, Charlotte. And you know damn well, there's nothing out there like it."

"Done. And I need it wrapped like the infant Jesus. It's going abroad."

"Net" was the friendly discount off the list price that dealers gave all designers. "Net net" was the even friendlier discount given to favorite designers. Depending on the item, the discounts ran anywhere from a conservative 10% or 20% all the way up to 30% and 40%. Charlotte, of course, never settled for less than net net. Occasionally, she would pass on some of the discount to her clients. Other times, considering what she had to put up with servicing these clients, she figured that she was more than entitled to keep the "change."

After neatly avoiding a farewell hug, Charlotte stood out on the street and hailed a cab. Fastening her seatbelt, she gave the driver, Ahmed, the address for her home on North Moore and decided to let him find his own way down. As they crawled across 72nd to Fifth (*Bad choice! Bad choice!* she whispered furiously under her breath) she thought about Pavel.

He was the only client she rarely ripped off. You didn't screw Russians. Except maybe in the biblical sense. Which reminded her... That wasn't a bad idea. With his wife and kids stuck out in the suburbs of Jersey ("It's safer for them there," he'd said), they might make a great couple. Unlike the powerful men in New York for whom money had become an abstract; men whose eyes were as dull as their edge after years of board meetings, distant wives, and charity benefits, Pavel was still sharp. He lived on the cusp of chaos and the brink of collapse. Experiencing that chaos, even vicariously, was a thrill. When she'd been with him that night at Anna's, the night he'd asked her to redo the dacha, she'd felt both irresistibly alive and afraid.

14

Charlotte felt her neck snap when the cabdriver slammed on the brakes.

"Asshole," she screamed as the driver hit the gas and her body bounced back against the seat. They'd been lurching down Fifth Avenue for twenty-five minutes. Traffic was so snarled up, it was nearly at a standstill. She could see the flashing lights and Con Ed truck parked in the middle of the avenue ahead.

"I'm getting out," she yelled as the cab reached the corner of 23rd Street "Now!"

Pumping the brakes, the driver turned around and flashed her an enormous grin.

"First day!" he said, as proud as if he just announced the birth of a son.

"Well, good luck!" Charlotte replied, flinging him a twenty and pushing the back door open. "You'll need it!"

Other people were popping up umbrellas. But Charlotte liked the sensation of soft, light rain on her face. Picking up speed and finding her rhythm, she strode west towards the river.

Charlotte refused to use what she called "ear gear" on her walks: no Bluetooths, iPods or cell phones. They interfered with those rare moments of communion that she felt with the city.

Despite efforts to live a life laid out in ruler-straight lines, Charlotte was constantly careening between wild extremes. She knew no middle ground. Here in New York and only here did even street signs speak to her in terms of those extremes:

"Don't even think of parking here!"

"Get off the grass!"

"Don't litter. It's selfish."

This was language that Charlotte understood. It was intimate and personal. It wasted no time in cutting her, and everyone else in town, down to size.

This was the wonderful thing about New York. It was bigger than Charlotte. And somehow, she found comfort in that. This city was, for her, what religion was to others.

She *believed* in it. No matter how dwarfed or diminished she might occasionally feel by its experience, no matter how her own hopes might have dwindled, she couldn't abandon it. It was the only place in the world that she'd ever felt she belonged.

Sticking to the pedestrian path along the river, as a blur of bikes and skaters swooshed past her, Charlotte remembered her first night in her loft. There had been a shootout between two Polish antiques dealers across the street. "The sound of gunfire was like Jiffy Pop," she'd told Vicky later. "When the kernels are so hot, they start exploding up against the tin foil." It was hard to believe that such an innocuous sound could be so lethal. But one guy was lying under a canopy across from her building, bleeding to death. The other guy had limped to the end of the street and collapsed on the corner of North Moore and Hudson. He'd been shot in the neck and lungs.

"My God! Charlotte," Vicky had gasped when she heard the story. "How can you possibly stay there another minute? I mean, why don't you move uptown? "

Unlike Vicky, who ventured downtown even less often than she ventured into her own $500,000 kitchen, Charlotte wouldn't have dreamed of moving. The murders were just another chapter in the city's story of extremes; an experience that brought Charlotte closer to the soul of this place—a place that never failed to embrace and console her.

By the time she walked over the bridge and crossed the West Side Highway, the early autumn twilight had turned to dark. She could still hear the creaking of swings in the new children's park across Washington Street and the murmur of mothers' voices as they gave their kids a final push, cajoling them towards home with promises of dinner and bedtime stories.

Charlotte felt herself tumbling into a familiar limbo. The feeling was similar to catching one's heel on the edge of a rug. She was losing her balance, falling. Caught in the beginnings of that lethargy and listlessness that signaled depression, she felt almost homeless. Turning her key in the lock, she entered the apartment.

For the first time in months, Charlotte didn't fight it. She simply allowed the void to engulf her. Lying prone on the living room couch as the inertia rolled over her and her muscles and mind went slack, even the impulse to breathe seemed to demand too much effort. When she was younger, much younger, Charlotte had often feared that this oppressively flat and featureless inner landscape would drive her mad. It was a sign of weakness, a shameful secret, that she'd hidden away while practicing her smile in the bathroom mirror.

But even now, she was glad that she'd cut down on her antidepressants. She missed the vertiginous highs after these periods of inertia—a state of being, or non-being—that Charlotte also likened to being buried alive. She was picturing herself at the airport with Amy's set of custom-made Vuitton when her world went dark.

15

She still wasn't used to the new electric toothbrush. Every

time, she switched it on, she felt as if she were brushing with a swarm of mosquitoes or bees in her mouth. After rinsing and tying her hair back in a ponytail, she strode off towards the kitchen. Cleaning was one of Charlotte's pre-mission rituals. It was also one of her greatest pleasures. She found a certain nobility in the work.

Her supplies were in a closet next to the Sub-Zero refrigerator. Slipping her hands into a pair of pink rubber gloves, she filled a pail with hot, steamy water and vinegar and rolled up her sleeves. *Why is this work so satisfying*, she wondered before getting down on her hands and knees to scrub the grouting between the Italian tiles with an old toothbrush. *Maybe it's the physical part of it,* she thought. "*Sweat equity.*" Wielding mops, dusting, ironing clothes, and washing floors was a means of claiming a space as one's own. It created a complicity between the animate and the inanimate. It brought a house alive.

Sitting back with her hands on her hips, she pitied all the women in New York who never touched a broom, a mop, an iron, a sponge. Women who only sweat in spas and private gyms in front of personal trainers. ("Gymnausea," she called it.)

After mopping the floors and wiping down the window ledges with more hot water and vinegar, she placed two fresh lemon wedges in the dishwasher and reached for the Dustbuster. This one was so powerful, it even sucked up liquids. It had been a Christmas present from her ex-boyfriend, Paul. "How can you stand being such a neat freak?" he'd asked her as she unwrapped the gift. "You're so neurotically tidy!"

What did slobs like Paul know of such primal,

uncomplicated joys? Of a woman's deep, unfulfilled longings not just for order but for the dazzle, the spotless promise of new beginnings? This was the pleasure of cleaning house, this aura of promise.

After replacing the Dustbuster in its charger, Charlotte smiled. She could smell the scent of lemon from the dishwasher. She'd reline the cabinets later with a new, hand-waxed paper from Kate's Paperie. The only job that remained was the poker. Opening up the cabinet beneath the kitchen sink, she pulled out a can of Brasso and her soft chamois cloth. Nothing cleaned better than old-fashioned elbow grease.

16

Shit! The prong of the poker was stuck, like the barb of a fish hook in the woman's skull. "Hard-headed *mother*!" Charlotte snarled as she wriggled the poker around, hoping to cajole it free. Nothing. Spreading her legs while taking a deep, cleansing breath, she focused and gave it one more brutal tug. The poker tore free, flinging a piece of scalp and $600 worth of streaked, blonde hair against a closet door.

Right up until this last little hitch, everything had gone like clockwork. Despite the pouring rain, Charlotte had appeared at the townhouse and rang the bell at 4. She was always punctual. "It isn't just a question of being polite," her mother had drummed into her. "It's a sign of respect for the other person, dear." Dressed in a Searle parka, black leggings and a leotard, and toting a big black bag with her new neon pink yoga mat, she looked just like every other Upper East Side trophy wife returning from a workout.

"Yes, yes, who is it?" came the scratchy voice from the intercom.

"It's Coreen, from Craigslist," she replied, keeping her head hidden in the hood of her parka.

"Oh all right," the impatient voice sounded put out. "Just a minute."

Convinced that the house would be fully staffed, Charlotte was relieved to see only the petite, infuriated blonde, dressed in head-to-toe pink Chanel, who opened the massive black door.

"Everybody, I mean *everybody*, is at the house in Bedford," she informed Charlotte in a clipped voice. "I've had to shut the whole security system down myself."

"Oh dear! You poor thing," Charlotte replied, sidling into the foyer before the young woman could change her mind.

"You have no idea how complicated the system is... All the zones and cameras and sirens..."

"Is it off?" Charlotte asked.

"Yes!" Amy said. "But only after I was forced to spend twenty minutes on the phone with some mentally impaired imbecile at the security company."

"I know just how frustrating that can be," Charlotte said, inching her way past a fabulous 17th century oak table in the hallway.

"It's also the biggest gala of the year for the Fashion Group," the woman huffed and puffed. "I'm on the committee and my personal stylist called in sick."

"Well, I won't take long, I promise." Charlotte said.

"Fine. But I have to be dressed and ready in an hour," Amy said, turning on her red-soled Louboutins and heading for the marble staircase.

"I'm just curious, Amy. Why do you advertise on Craigslist?" Charlotte asked as the woman click-clacked her way up the stairs. "I mean, you don't seem like the type."

"My husband asked me the same question," Amy said with a laugh. "He said, 'It's a bit lowbrow, don't you think, darling?' But I told him I was setting an example. I'll give the money to charity, naturally."

Naturally, Charlotte mimicked to herself.

"I call it recycling," Amy said. "You know, doing my bit for a sustainable world?"

"Well, I think it's admirable," Charlotte replied, massaging the tiny woman's mammoth ego.

Following in Amy's cushioned footsteps (the museum-quality Persians were priceless), Charlotte swept past a series of cluttered rooms with cathedral ceilings, staid but safe and expensive "brown" or English oak furniture, and chintz. Christ! So much chintz.

Signature Marietta, Charlotte sniffed, disdainfully thinking of the designer. *The King of Queens.*

"My husband's first wife had the *worst* taste." Amy said, as if reading her mind. "But she was still, *you know*, 'in the picture' when we first got together, so I haven't been able to change things as fast as I've wanted. Richard says his kids need a slower transition. Anyway, we're redoing everything this summer," she added smugly. "I'm working with Stephen and we're thinking about going totally retro. You know, Hollywood Regency?"

Argh!

The bedroom was a nightmare of pink and red toile de Jouy—window treatments, canopies, even the walls of the 1,500-square foot dressing room were covered with Jouy. The four-piece Vuitton luggage had been dumped into a corner, near one of the closets under a dry cleaner's rolling rack.

"There it is," Amy said, pointing with her index finger. "I only used it once, on my honeymoon, two years ago. It's just been gathering dust up here."

"It's exquisite," Charlotte said, moving in closer to admire the luster of the hand-tooled brown leather and the brass work.

"I see the trunk is locked. Is there a key or..."

"Yes. Obviously there's a key."

"For three thousand dollars, I'd like to look at the inside if you don't mind."

"Oh, really!" Amy said, expelling an exasperated sigh. "I'll have to see if it's in the drawer here."

Turning her back, she began sorting through a drawer of neatly rolled up, hand pressed, $350 silk underpants.

Charlotte slid the poker out from inside the yoga mat in her bag.

"I'm going to have Vuitton make me..."

Charlotte grinned as the heavy brass poker slid ever so smoothly into the back of Amy's neatly groomed head. A startled "Oh" of surprise, a whoosh of bad breath, and the woman crumpled to the floor. Charlotte hit her again.

When the jerking stopped, she crouched down on her well-toned haunches and gave the body a quick kick. A single tear spilled down an implanted cheek. Both eyes were open. Walking into the bathroom, Charlotte removed a Handi Wipe from her bag, turned on the faucet, and rinsed the poker in the tub. She also checked her garments for blood. Certain that she hadn't touched anything but the poker with her bare hands, she shut off the faucet with the Handi Wipe, and trotted back into the dressing room.

As she crept around the pool of blackened liquid that had begun to soak through the white wall-to-wall carpet, the deep richness of the color reminded her of those luscious old oil-based Dutch enamel paints. You couldn't even buy them anymore in New York. "People worry about the fumes," some guy at the Janovic paint store had told her with a shrug of his shoulders. She had to order them from England now. Tugging on the handle of the Vuitton trunk, Charlotte sighed. "What a waste! There's no way I can heave this home alone." Instead, Charlotte picked up the vanity case, slung her bag over her shoulder, and casually retraced her steps to the foyer. The phone was ringing.

Within hours, this place would be crawling with cops, gaping at everything from the marble staircase and 16-foot Flemish tapestries to the deserted chintz-filled salons. Cops who, if they were lucky and worked hours of overtime every week, just managed to pay the mortgages on ranch houses in Jersey and on Long Island. As they fumbled through layers of frilly $350 silk underpants, would they think of their own tired, frazzled wives? Wives who could only afford to dream of a long three-day weekend in Cancun? Charlotte imagined the cops going through the motions more meticulously than usual due to the victim's identity.

Paper bagging her hands, they would hope that she'd fought off her assailant and that her fingernails would reveal traces of blood or hair. They'd check the drains, the traps in the bathroom and run the tapes from the security cameras. All for nothing, Charlotte had left a message on the woman's cell phone. True. But that was two days ago. Who saves messages for two whole days? And she'd called from a payphone, anyway. They'd dust for nonexistent prints, get a hold of the woman's land-line phone records, and take a million digital photos of the "crime scene."

Hell, they might even haul out the tub and rip off the metal section of the door frame downstairs, looking for "ridge detail prints." She'd read about that in the *Post* after the murder of Linda Stein, the punk rap manager turned Realtor to the stars. She'd been killed by her own personal assistant, news that Charlotte believed had come as a terrible shock to everyone in the city except the thousands of other personal assistants who dreamed, daily, of doing the same thing.

But Charlotte respected these cops. Unlike the rest of humanity, these detectives would spend days trying to get under her skin and inside her head—to walk around in her shoes. If they were smart and dedicated, they would get closer to her than anyone else. Because the toughest, most successful cops were also brilliantly intuitive and empathic.

Using the sleeve of her Searle parka, Charlotte twisted open the front doorknob, glanced out at the empty street, and sauntered off into a torrential downpour. *Rain is good*, Charlotte thought to herself as she pulled up her hood and ducked down low to avoid the eye of the CCTV camera next door. Usually, Charlotte was uncannily observant and attuned to her surroundings. But in her hurry, she missed the graffiti on the big blue mailbox. "Doom! Gloom! Boom! Soon!" read the anonymous message. She also missed the twitch of a white glass curtain on the first floor of a nearby townhouse.

17

Charlotte devoted the rest of her weekend to quality personal time. Late Sunday afternoon, she toted her trophies into the bathroom and set them up like a display of wedding gifts on top of her tiger maple cosmetic table. Running the bath with water as hot as she could stand, she stepped in and lay back, gazing at her hard-won acquisitions: the bottle of vintage Dom, the gold charm bracelet and the Vuitton. Her anxiety had given way to a sense of free floating ease, a mild euphoria that seemed to loosen her every muscle. All of the static, the incessant chatter inside her head, had gone as silent as the city after a heavy snowfall.

If only these women had the courage to see their own small, unhappy lives as she did, Charlotte thought. *They'd be grateful to her.* She was doing them a favor, releasing them from their misery. Reaching over for a neatly creased copy of the *Post*, she reread the feature story.

MANSION MAMA MURDERED!

By Ben Volpone

Sources close to the Manhattan Police Commissioner's office report that the Friday afternoon murder of 28-year-old Amy Webb, wife of Richard Webb, one of the city's hottest bond traders, has officials desperately seeking leads.

"The security system, including cameras and motion detectors, was off. There were no signs of forced entry," the source informed a *Post* reporter. "But there are distinct similarities between this case and other unsolved female homicides in Manhattan." When pressured for details, the source refused to elaborate. The police commissioner will speak at a press conference Monday afternoon.

Amy Webb, a small town girl born in the hills of western Pennsylvania, worked briefly as Mr. Webb's personal assistant prior to their society wedding in Palm Beach, two years ago. The wedding, attended by the famous and infamous alike, made local headlines when Kanye West, the new Mrs. Webb's favorite rapper, dedicated his song about prenups and gold diggers to the blushing bride. According to Palm Beach newspapers, "The groom was not amused."

Webb's body was discovered in her dressing room by her husband when he returned home early from a Fashion Group benefit at which his wife had failed to appear. Calls for comments to his office on Wall Street and his home in Bedford were not returned.

Charlotte put down the paper and began soaping her

body with a loofah. She thought about how little the world would miss these women. Like Vicky, they were predators, her so-called "victims." Even more depressing, these same women would give birth to children who would grow up equally delusional. Children, like Charlotte, who would be orphaned by their mother's hollow-hearted, venomous ambitions.

Finishing up her spa ritual with a Clarins facial and a thirty-minute Klorane hair treatment, she reached for a bath sheet. Unfortunately, her most determined efforts to thwart her own mother's plan to drop by for afternoon tea had failed miserably. "I'm bringing you a gift," she'd shouted into the telephone. "Don't even think of trying to cancel." Why did deaf people shout, anyway? It wasn't as if Charlotte was the one who was hard of hearing.

From the minute her mother had set foot in the door, her visit had gone downhill. "What a pity Parke Bernet went out of business, dear," she'd said, eyeing the bold geometric pattern of Charlotte's favorite Caucasian carpet. "I mean, I do *so* prefer old Persians, don't you?"

When the two sat down on her new slipcovered couch, the sniping resumed. "And these pillows, Charlotte. What on earth possessed you?"

Charlotte loved the shock of oversize pink peonies set against black and white striped cotton. They were a stroke of genius. "They're so unbearably *loud*," her mother had added, shifting her body sideways, as if to remove herself from the offensive burst of color. "I'm not really criticizing, darling. We all have different ways of expressing ourselves, don't we?"

Charlotte twitched and changed the subject. "You look

beautiful, Mother," she had said, hoping to deflect the insults. And it worked.

Pursing her lips in a semblance of a smile, her mother had no choice but to thank her. The thing is, she *did* look beautiful.

Long before women began to age so disgracefully; before "lethal injections" like Botox, Sculptra, and collagen, her mother was having facials twice a month and shielding her skin from the sun with hats and silk umbrellas. Neither the treasonous betrayals brought about by age or experience had touched her mother. Even at sixty-two years old, her skin remained luminously white and unblemished. So why did she continue to taunt and belittle her daughter? And what is it that made Charlotte so eager to please this woman who gave so little back?

Charlotte had always tried to be the perfect child: obedient, polite, responsible. But this undermining had been going on for as long as she could remember. Even when Charlotte succeeded, she sensed that she was, somehow, slipping. Always slipping.

Sometimes, it was physical—the sensation. A split second fit of dizziness. A moment when she was unsure of her footing. How dare her mother attack her in such a private, vulnerable place? Somebody had once said that decorating was a form of dreaming out loud. Charlotte agreed. But it was only here, within the safety of her own home, that she had ever permitted herself to fully explore those dreams. Yet still she smiled at her mother. It hurt her face, the smiling.

"Smile! Charlotte! Smile!" her mother would snarl, tugging her by the hand when she was small and looking straight into whatever lens seemed to be pointed in their direction. They were usually leaving Serendipity or Gino's after an early Sunday night dinner. Only Charlotte seemed to understand that the papps had no interest in them. They were often just blocking the shot of some famous person behind them.

If she didn't smile quickly enough, or the photographers ignored them, her mother would blame her. "No one likes a sourpuss," she'd sneer, yanking her by the hair and dragging her towards a dingy maid's room at home. It was off the kitchen. The bed had been removed and the only light came from a grated vent that overlooked an airshaft. "You can come out when you've learned to behave yourself," she'd say, leaving Charlotte locked in the dark. How she'd dreaded the sound of her mother's heels fading into the distance.

Any infraction of her mother's rules, including touching her after she had finished dressing for her evenings out, and Charlotte was exiled to the room. It wasn't easy, fighting the impulse to caress the yards of creamy silk or satin that her mother wore as lightly as she did the deliriously heavy scent of Joy. At first, the experience in the room was terrifying. But then, she'd close her eyes and begin to sing. Over the years, she'd also furnished the room with things that comforted her: a coarse blue blanket, a bottle of water, her Paddington Bear. She refused to bring in a flashlight or even a book of matches. Instead, Charlotte trained herself to embrace the fear; to become one with the darkness.

As she'd unwrapped her gift, a curious poster-like package, she'd wished that her mother could have read her mind. *Why am I always tongue-tied with you?* She was asking herself.

Why, at thirty-seven years old, haven't I learned to strike back? Just a glimpse of her gift—of the framed cartoon figure and Charlotte was shaking.

"I found this in the attic out in..."

Her mother was kneading her hands in her lap. "In," she said again, while rubbing the fabric of the couch.

Charlotte looked at her, puzzled. "In Alpine, Mother?"

"Of course, dear. Where else?" Her mother snapped. "Remember how many of these you used to draw?"

The figure had black stick-like legs, a round, striped body, and a face shaped like the letter C. The inside of the C revealed row after row of sharp, pointed teeth—an open mouth, caught in an enraged, silent howl. Funny how her mother had detested the drawings back then. Now she was pulling them out from the attic and showing them off. But why had she drawn such a strange blank and fumbled for that one word? Alpine had been her home for over twenty years.

"Well, darling ... what do you say?" her mother had asked, swinging her thick, chestnut-red hair, with its bold silver streaks, back from her face. "I thought you might be touched by the gesture."

"I am. Thank you," Charlotte replied as she tore her eyes away from the cartoon.

Disobeying her mother had never come easily to Charlotte. Her singing, for instance, had been reduced to a barely audible hum after her mother's order to stop. But she did remember the forbidden trips to the attic that began after her sister died. The hours she'd spent idly talking to snapshots of relatives she'd never met. The one she liked best was of a pudgy, overdressed woman standing on a boardwalk by the sea. There was a giant Ferris wheel behind her. "My sister, Dottie, Orchard Beach, 1952," it said on the back. Charlotte slipped it into her pants one afternoon and hid it in the pages of a book in her bedroom. The photo now sat in a silver frame next to her bed. It was along with these surreptitious visits to the attic after her sister's death that Charlotte had also begun drawing the "C men." Deliberately pushing the memory of that recurring horror with her sister out of her mind, she had dutifully thanked her mother before escorting her to a taxi. "I have a headache," her mother announced, wearily. "I need to go to sleep."

Her mother had suffered from migraines all her life. When she'd received the perfunctory rejection letter from Shinnecock Golf Club and the Union League in New York, she'd gone to bed for three days. "She's in mourning," her father had said, sarcastically. "Don't go near her."

The replay of her mother's visit during her bath had left her so irritated and impatient, Charlotte decided to walk a few blocks before bed. Lacing up her Nikes and grabbing a Burberry parka, she locked the door and headed for the elevator. A fierce wind was blowing in from the river as she hit the street and walked down to Duane and Washington.

"Hey, Charlotte! Charlotte!" It was John, the homeless man. "Got a dollar? Got a dollar?" Not only was John accustomed to people looking straight through him, nobody listened to him, either. Maybe this was why he always repeated himself. Shuffling towards her with his shopping bag clutched against his chest, he was dressed in his usual uniform: khaki pants, a cloth coat, and a button-down Oxford shirt. When he put down his shopping bag, she smiled and passed him a ten. There was something positively patrician about John. Even the way he spoke, the way he said "Yah! Yah!" reminded her of George Plimpton.

Twenty-five minutes later, Charlotte snuggled in between her new Pratesi sheets and thought about John. Every day, rain or shine, he took the subway down from a shelter on 118th Street and hung around on the same corner. Why had he chosen this corner? What made it feel like home? Was he simply a creature of habit? The whole neighborhood, everyone who fed him and paid for his coffee and winter boots, wondered what had made him snap and begin living on the streets.

Just before dawn, Charlotte sat bolt upright, shivering, her body slick with sweat. She hadn't had this nightmare in years. She was leaping over rooftops, her mouth open in a rictus-like O of fear, too scared to even scream. Her mother, dressed to kill in a twin set and pearls, was chasing after her, holding a kitchen knife.

18

The question was right there under "Just Asking" on Page Six of the *Post*. "Just Asking" was the IQ test of gossip. Salacious snippets of info about the behavior of nameless celebutards, socialites, and players offered in the form of thinly veiled questions. If you were connected, you guessed who among the high (like, *very high*) and mighty was off to rehab, sleeping around, losing their jobs, whatever. But today's question deviated from the usual format:

> Is there a "web Webb" connection?
>
> How did Amy Webb's killer gain access to her East Side mansion? Could it have been a chat room encounter gone tragically wrong? Is it some Internet connection that links the murder of this oh-so-well-to-do socialite with other wealthy female victims in Manhattan? We're just asking...

Charlotte looked at her caller ID and picked up the phone. It was Anna's usual Monday morning breakfast call. Ordinarily, after a mission, Charlotte would have been delighted to listen to Anna's gossip about the murder. She imagined that it was like enjoying a cigarette after sex. But her mother's Sunday visit and the nightmare had robbed her of even that tiny pleasure. So instead, Charlotte ranted on about her Sunday afternoon.

"Charlotte. Listen to me, please," Anna said, cutting her off. "I know I sound like that guy with the ears in *Star Wars*. What was his name?"

Charlotte felt a tickle in the back of her throat. She giggled. There had been a particularly depressing night during the summer when Anna had showed up at her door with a bottle of Veuve and forced her to watch the entire Star Wars trilogy. "Yoda. His name was Yoda," she replied, twisting a strand of hair around her pinkie finger.

"Yoda, si. But people only have as much power as you give them. Do you understand what I'm saying?"

"Of course, I understand, Anna. And that's very wise. But I can't help it. I feel sorry for her. And I hate her. It's all mixed up."

Anna laughed. "Do you know why your mother is so good at pushing your buttons, Charlotte?"

"I'm not in the mood for jokes, Anna."

"Because she installed them. I read that in a book somewhere."

The joke worked. Charlotte felt as if someone had let the air out of her. Her shoulders slumped with the release of tension as she walked over from the table to steam the milk for her cappuccino.

"There is one more step in my therapy session, Charlotte. You must tell me a funny story about your parents, please..."

Charlotte gazed, bleakly, at the pale aqua walls and delft blue trim in her kitchen. Humor was not something she associated with her parents. But Anna was one of the most persistent women Charlotte had ever known.

"I'm not hanging up until you tell me, Charlotte."

Racking her brain, Charlotte heaped two spoonfuls of sugar into her coffee. "Okay. I may have one story," she conceded. "It didn't seem funny at the time, but now..."

"Go ahead," Anna coaxed. "I'm lighting a cigarette. I'm ready."

Charlotte wiped the creamy froth from her upper lip with the back of her hand. "I was eight years old," she said. "I woke up one night and my mother was yelling at my father. 'Ben! Ben! Wake up!' When I snuck out of bed, I saw him swinging an invisible golf club at the top of the stairs. He was sleepwalking his way through eighteen holes, Anna."

Anna giggled. "You see how it helps?"

"Sure," Charlotte replied, burning her tongue on the hot coffee. What she didn't tell Anna was that the golf incident happened three months after her little sister had died. All Charlotte remembered about that time in her life was her own feelings of rejection. It had hurt her, too. The loss of the baby. After all, she was the one who had gotten up that night to comfort her when she was crying. She'd even turned her over on her stomach and left with her own Paddington Bear for company.

Her cell phone trilled.

"I have to go, Anna," she said, eager to avoid more questions. She loved Anna for asking questions. But she felt guilty about hiding things. Like the fact that she'd had to schedule a doctor's appointment after the sonogram.

"Everything's fine. Just a little indigestion," she'd lied when her friend asked about the results. Anna had been elated.

"Don't forget Max at 1!" she was saying. "I sold my soul to get you that meeting."

"I won't," Charlotte replied. Max was the city's most infamous Gothic and Renaissance furniture dealer. For twenty years, he'd refused to allow 'drekerators' into his store. Picking up her cell, she swore quietly to herself. It was Rita again.

"Charlotte? I'm worried about the pool. There's not a lot of time between now and the beginning of the season."

"It'll be done, Rita. I promise."

"Well, you should have called to let me know," Rita snapped.

"I'm on my way right now to talk with the landscape architect," Charlotte lied.

"I want you to have a chat with our new real estate manager," Rita replied. Charlotte let out an audible sigh. "He can handle hiring the contractors. And I'll expect to see the plans when we meet on Saturday."

The phone went dead. Rita had fired two real estate managers in the past year. Responsible for maintaining the family yacht, the jet, and the eight homes the Brickmans owned, it was a job from hell, even with five assistants. Busying herself near the stove, Charlotte chopped up heirloom tomatoes and a bit of French gruyere for a breakfast omelet. When the butter sizzled in the pan, she threw in three whisked eggs and flashed backed to her last visit to the Vineyard. It was in the spring.

Rita had "imported" four "in-help" from the city, all Ecuadorian. They spoke very little English and Rita herself hadn't yet spent enough time in Cabo to learn even the few words necessary to order them around. When Charlotte arrived from the airport, she'd stood unseen in the foyer while her client reamed out a terrified-looking twenty-year-old girl in the living room.

"You do not make de-ci-sions!" she screamed at the top of her lungs, pronouncing every syllable. "I make the de-ci-sions here! And we do not ever use *this* wax in our house!"

The girl timidly nodded her head up and down in a desperate attempt to appear as if she understood.

"Go, go!" Rita screamed. "Back to the kitchen. And don't forget to fill the ice trays with FIJI water!"

Charlotte was so embarrassed that she was afraid to say hello. But Rita had seen her.

"Sorry, Charlotte," she said with a laugh, as she walked over for a hug. "Help just isn't what it used to be."

Folding the tomatoes in with the eggs, that last bit still made Charlotte giggle. *How the hell would Rita know anything about what help used to be?* Charlotte wondered as she slid the omelet from her pan onto a white Wedgewood plate. *The woman had* no *help till twelve years ago.*

It was her mentor, Harold, who had introduced Charlotte to the Brickmans. "They exhaust me," he'd said. "So I'll take on the project, but you do most of the work. You'll make plenty of money, don't worry."

The fifteen room duplex in a Fifth Avenue building was one of Charlotte's first projects as a designer. It was also the project that earned her the nickname, "the halo from hell." Harold's partner had eventually accused her not just of stealing thousands in kickbacks due to Harold from millworkers and other subcontractors, but of stealing the client, too. Which was ridiculous, Charlotte had protested to Harold.

It wasn't her fault if the Brickmans fell in love with her. She'd done everything she possibly could to discourage them from dropping him. Even if Harold had seemed disappointed at the time, he hadn't gotten angry or refused to speak to her. Not like his partner, Miles. But this was ancient history. As ancient as people's perceptions that Jews like the Brickmans didn't live in New York's toniest buildings or own homes on Nantucket and the Vineyard.

"Dear God! Charlotte!" one of New York's newly impoverished Wasps had said to her, as he slurred his way through a third dirty Bombay gin martini at the Brook Club the previous week. "My grandfather would be rotating in his grave at the idea of mezuzahs in Maine and Martha's Vineyard. I mean, Martha Stewart in Seal Harbor was bad enough... But Jews??? Or how about those gay guys? I've heard they've bought half of Mt. Desert."

Even as a non-practicing half-Jew, Charlotte writhed in her club chair. *Addlepated little toad!* she'd thought to herself. "You have no idea how forgotten you are."

Because the bottom line (metaphorically speaking), was that this generation of new money, Jews or not, didn't give a damn about Wasps who belonged to the Brook or the Union Club, and lived off their meager interest from ironclad trust funds. They would guffaw all the way to the Caymans at the idea of waiting in a room marked "STRANGERS" like the one Charlotte had once sat in at the Park Avenue Racquet and Tennis Club, while a porter went to fetch a member.

Rinsing the Wedgewood in warm soapy water reminded Charlotte, once again, of Rita and her problems with the pool.

Christ! The pool! Charlotte shuddered at the prospect of that discussion. Rita had only learned to swim three summers earlier—in the arms of an Olympic swimming coach, of course. This was shortly after they'd finished construction on the 15,000-square-foot "cottage" in Gay Head, the uber exclusive area of the Vineyard where Jackie O once had her place. A neo-Victorian monstrosity with faux Gothic turrets and "trim," Rita claimed it was a tribute to the island's whaling widows.

"More like wailing with an 'i,'" Charlotte had laughed with Anna later. But she couldn't deny that the project was a huge success.

Architectural Digest had given the interiors six full pages. *The World of Inferiors*, as Charlotte had now renamed England's poshest shelter mag, turned it down. "Not modern enough, dear," the editor had e-mailed her. Even if Charlotte herself was sick to death of Hitchcock and Shaker chairs and hutches, of authentic colonial grape presses and milk-paint pie cupboards, she couldn't help but appreciate what they'd done to her bank balance.

What a travesty! Charlotte thought, as she hurriedly rifled through the hangers in her cedar-lined, 200-square-foot walk-in closet. All these people paying thousands of dollars for stuff designed by the Shakers. How many Shakers depended on lifestyle management teams and personal assistants and concierges and hot-rock massages to get through their day?

19

There it was. No sign, of course. The windows were so thick with soot and dust, Charlotte could hardly see inside. Cupping her hands on the side of her face, she peered in at the bizarre mix of trash and treasure: half-chewed dog bones, a ripped tapestry-covered wing chair, and small polychrome angels with wings wide open, suspended in midair.

"Whatcha doin'?" The voice startled her. It sounded like that old dead actor, Jimmy Cagney, raspy and pure Bronx. Turning around, Charlotte found herself face-to-face with the legendary 5' 3" dealer himself.

"I'm Anna's friend, Charlotte," she said, reaching out to shake hands.

"Yeah! I heard about ya!" he said, returning the handshake. "Another drekerator, right?"

"Right, Max," Charlotte said mildly. Bouncing around on the balls of his feet like a boxer in the ring, Max had a head of wavy black hair and the shrewdest pair of brown eyes that she'd ever seen. He was chewing on the stump of a dead cigar. "Least, ya don't look like one them broads born in the back of a Town Car. And I don't see no monogram on your canvas tote bag, neither."

"No, Max. That's never been my style," Charlotte said.

"Ya gonna buy?" he asked, with an impish grin.

"Yes, I am!" Charlotte said. "I've been waiting to buy from you for fifteen years, Max."

Max hoisted up the metal gates, pushed the two-foot-thick wooden door open and gestured her inside.

Through the gloom, gold glittered. Burnished gold on six-foot pricket sticks, ornate Spanish picture frames, and Venetian mirrors with glass, wavy and pocked with age. The furniture: armoires, prie-dieus, throne-like chairs, gleamed with that dull, polished patina that came only from centuries' worth of hands gently rubbing the surface.

Whose hands? Charlotte wondered. There were statues of saints and of the Madonna and more angels than in most cathedrals.

"I'm in heaven," Charlotte sighed.

"You're in hell," Max replied. "I haven't sold a thing in months."

This was one of the many mysteries about Max. Anna said that if he sold his inventory at even pennies on the dollar, he'd be a multimillionaire. Instead he lived like a pauper in the back of the storefront with a one-eyed cat and a decrepit golden retriever.

"I'm warnin' ya," Max said. "I don't want ya in here buyin' stuff cuz it looks good with the wallpaper, cuz it fits in with the color of the fuckin' carpet."

"Guess we're not off to a great start, here, huh?" Charlotte countered with a smile. "Fact is, I don't care how you feel about me or my profession. I'm here to buy for my best client."

"Sorry, sorry," he said. "Guess I'm just not used to customers. Go ahead. Take a walk. There's more stuff downstairs."

"Thanks," Charlotte said, resisting the impulse to race toward the back and begin exploring. Thirty minutes later, tiptoeing around a painted Venetian chest, its lacquered red Chinoiserie faded pink with age, her eyes lit up at the sight of a ten-foot wooden cassa panca. The back of the Italian bench/chest was painted with figures of Botticelli-like full bodied women and bearded men in velvet robes. It was a fantastic piece. Pavel, her Russian, would love it.

The lights blinked twice. "Hey!" Max shouted. "Ya still alive?"

"Sorry, Max. I got lost," Charlotte answered, taking a last lingering look at the piece. "I'm coming."

"So whaddya lookin' at?" he said with a squint as Charlotte

appeared from downstairs, wiping the dust off her hands.

Charlotte told him.

"Well, whaddya know!" he said, "The lady's got taste."

"Don't bother with the flattery, Max. It's wasted on me."

"Last person looked seriously at that piece was Eye-talian. A Roman dealer buyin' for some fancy-pants movie actor on Lake Como."

George Clooney. Charlotte thought. "Here's the thing, Max. I'm going to pay you what it's worth. I'm not even going to haggle."

She could see the glee in his eyes. "And all I want in return is the truth. I want to know everything there is to know about the provenance, the whole history, OK? Where you got it, when, from whom, everything."

"OK. How's 600 Gs sound to ya?"

He was testing her. "Five hundred sounds better."

"Jeez. That's just about right. But you'd pay another hundred if you was buyin' it in Europe."

"So let's split the difference. I'll give you an extra fifty," Charlotte replied, eyeing the bottle of Old Grand-Dad bourbon behind him.

"Shall we open it? Seal the deal?" asked Max.

"Sure. But I'm going to have to bring down my client. He's here next week. And you'll have to be nice to him, Max."

"No problem," Max said, blowing the dust off the bottle.

Over the next hour and two neat shots of bourbon, Charlotte listened, raptly, to the story of the chest. It was what Max (and all dealers) euphorically called "a sleeper." A sleeper was a piece that nobody recognized for what it really was and that could be worth hundreds of times more than what a dealer paid for it. Max had seen the cassa panca at an auction preview up at Sotheby's in the late '90s. Part of a collection from the estate of Iris Love, it was listed at an estimate of $10,000 to $15,000.

"When I first seen it," he said to Charlotte, rubbing his hands together in delight, "I couldn't believe it. It was like recognizin' some long lost relative you thought was dead." Unlike the experts at Sotheby's, who were only able to trace the piece back to the 1960s when Love had purchased it from a Paris dealer, Max knew more. Max had a photographic memory.

"It's 16th century, Charlotte. It was in the Ruspolli Palazzo in Rome!" He'd seen a photo of the piece in a vintage auction catalogue he was thumbing through on one of his many sleepless nights.

"I go back to the store that afternoon," Max said, throwing his head back and swallowing the last shot of bourbon, "And I pray. I wait for the day of the auction, hopin' to God nobody else recognizes it for what it really is."

Sure enough, Max got lucky. "It went for $9,500 plus the 10% buyer's premium," he said, raising his fist, triumphantly. "I had some guy from the Getty here to look at it two years ago. But they couldn't afford it."

"Their loss, my gain," Charlotte said, grinning as the phone rang.

"I gotta take this call," Max said, cupping his hand over the receiver.

"Let me know when your client's comin'. I liked meetin' ya."

Riding downtown on the subway, Charlotte didn't need to close her eyes or hum. She had been totally seduced by the charisma of Max's experience; by his defiance and his lonely but obsessive love for objects. Charlotte understood this connection. Tracing a relationship over hundreds of years between an object and those who had touched it, lived with it, and lost it meant more to Charlotte than any relationship with a human being ever would.

Climbing the stairs at Franklin Street she flipped open her phone and sighed. There were three messages from Vicky's number. She replayed them while walking towards Anna's shop on Duane Street. Each call was more hysterical than the last.

"Oh my God! Charlotte!" Vicky howled between sobs. "For Christ's sake, call me. Please. It's Phil."

Charlotte slowed down as she called back and waited for Vicky to pick up.

"Vicky, it's me. What the hell's the matter? Tell me!"

"I don't know what I'm going to do," Vicky wailed.

"Did Phil get hit by a bus? What?"

"He's having an affair, Charlotte. With some fucking Russian tart."

"I'm sure he's not, "Charlotte lied, remembering the titaness at the museum benefit. "Who told you?"

"He did, Charlotte. But he didn't know he was telling me."

"I don't get it," Charlotte said.

"It was his cell phone. It speed dialed me by accident when the bitch pushed him down on her bed. The phone must have been in his pocket."

"Oh my God! You've got to be kidding."

"I'm not kidding, Charlotte. I'm going to kill him. I invited that woman into my house for dinner last week. And today, I had to listen to them rolling around on the frigging mattress. Every time I slammed down my phone, it called me back. I could hear everything."

"Listen, Vicky. Hold tight. I'll be up tomorrow morning. Okay?"

"I don't know, Charlotte. I just don't know. How *could* he?"

Even if Vicky had never heard the gossip about "Phil Phil," which Charlotte sincerely doubted, why pull a tantrum now? She had six months to go before the second phase of her prenup kicked in. A phase that would involve what Vicky's lawyers had described as "a life-affecting sum." *None* was the only sum that Charlotte could imagine as truly "life-affecting" for Vicky. Hell, maybe Phil had dialed Vicky's number from the Russian's himself?

When the phone trilled again, she checked the number. No way she was going to talk to Vicky again until tomorrow. It was Anna.

"Charlotte, are you there?" she shrieked.

"Yes, I'm here. Stop shrieking, Anna."

"I just got a call from a friend. About the murder of that Webb woman!"

Charlotte's heart was pumping as if she'd been running. "Yeah. So what she'd say?"

"Ah Dio! Dio!" she said. "Cara, it may be the work of a serial killer!"

Charlotte could see Anna's hands, wildly acting out the drama while she spoke.

"I'll call you later, Anna. I'm on my way home." Snapping

the phone shut, Charlotte sprinted toward her loft on North Moore Street.

20

She'd missed New York News at 6. Only CNN had some footage with a few tantalizing sound bites. There were shots of Amy Webb at her wedding with her husband, of the divorcee with the Dom at the Whitney Biennale, and of the girl with the charm bracelet on some runway at a Paris fashion show. A brief close-up of the mayor and the police commissioner flanked by an army of flunkies was followed by the commissioner's statement.

"There is no reason for New Yorkers to panic. Yes, there are similarities. The victims are female, they died from blows to the head, and yes, as Ben at the *Post* pointed out, they seemed to be well-to-do. All we're asking right now is that the public be aware—"

"Sir, Sir! Is there a possibility that the murderer is using the Internet to get into these women's homes? Maybe through chat rooms or—"

"We're following up on several leads at the moment, Ben," replied the commissioner. "Forensic experts in the Computer Crime Squad will be working with detectives and—"

"But I heard—"

"Enough!" the mayor grabbed the mic. "To say any more at this point would be irresponsible. It's just too early in the investigation."

"When exactly will we know more, sir? When the next victim dies?"

The Mayor cast a withering look at the *Post* reporter and marched offstage with his army trailing closely behind him.

Snacking on a few slices of Parma proscuitto, some Gorgonzola and a beet salad, Charlotte walked into her home office and Googled "female serial killers." She hoped that she might find herself. Not by name, of course, but in additional stories that the search engine would have listed after the press conference. It was too early. She was soon lost in a sea of links.

According to one expert, female killers were more successful, more precise, more careful, and quieter than males. It took twice as long to catch them. Apparently, most females preferred to distance themselves from their victims by using poison, guns or some other means of physical separation during the killing. But Charlotte found a great deal of pleasure in her *proximity* to the women she killed. She felt a strange sense of intimacy with them. Sharing the moment of death, after all, was just about as intimate an experience as sex.

She then scrolled through the stuff about motives. The experts were way off here, too. She wasn't in it for the money, or control or sex and drugs. She was a mercy killer. She was liberating these women; freeing them from their 40-million-dollar, 12,000-square-foot golden cages.

The computer froze just as the phone rang. "Shit!" Charlotte whispered, picking it up while trying to reboot.

"Hey, Charlotte! It's Philip."

"Hello, Philip," she replied icily, thinking of Vicky's phone call.

"Listen, did you have to *kill* that broad for the bracelet?"

Charlotte's heart was pounding.

"I... I..." she stuttered.

"JK, Charlotte. JK, as my daughter says. But when I read in the *Post* about the connection between those murders and the Internet, I couldn't help but think of the bracelet you were wearing that night at the museum. You said you found it on Craigslist?"

"Yeah. Well, I don't find you even remotely funny, Philip," she said. "Plus you've been a total bastard to Vicky," she added as her pulse slowed and she caught her breath.

"I told her I'm going to make up for it. I want you to find a bracelet for her. And I'm taking her on safari. To Ted's bush camp in Botswana."

Everybody had heard about Ted the Billionaire's private camp in Botswana. He shared it with some sheik from the Emirates who flew in with a 747 full of falcons or something.

"That's nice, Philip. I just hope you leave your Russian at home."

"Ha! Ha! Charlotte," he said. "My masseur is here. Gotta go. Oh. I'm sure Tom told you he's coming with us, right?"

You mean my masseur, Charlotte said to herself, reminded of just how ungrateful they all were, including her so-called friends, Vicky and Tom. She hung up. Her head ached.

Charlotte usually resisted the impulse to take a sedative. They implied that she was weak, not in control. But the pills seemed to eliminate the nightmares. Chewing a milligram of Ativan, Charlotte waited for the sedative to take the edge off her anxiety. If a man as dumb as Phil had made a connection between the reports of an Internet killer and Craigslist, why hadn't the police? Surely they had read through the women's e-mails?

21

Charlotte had scheduled Tuesday and Wednesday for reviewing project costs with Darryl's architect, and choosing Pavel's fabric swatches at the 59th Street Decoration and Design building. Open to the trade only, the D&D was *the* resource for fabrics and furniture. It was also chock-a-block full of back-stabbing faux blonde *inferior* designers, and buzzed with vicious rumors and gossip. The so-called "Sporty Socials" were the worst. Oddly devoid of glamour, there was a certain thin-lipped ennui, a brittleness about these young girls that intrigued her.

She'd seen one of their latest projects in the final issue of *House & Garden*. It was a study in contorted edginess; so precious, so affected, Charlotte almost mourned the demise of chintz. "Exquisitely unlivable," Anna had said, grimly, while flipping through the six page lay-out.

Fingering a lush Scalamandre striped silk fabric (the list price was $1,500 a yard but she knew she'd get it for half that at net), Charlotte felt her phone vibrate.

"Where are you?" asked Vicky. "I really, really need you."

Charlotte signaled a girl over to cut a swatch.

"I'm at the D&D."

"Listen. I just wanted to thank you for being a shoulder to cry on yesterday."

"What are friends for?" Charlotte said, pointing the sales girl towards the silk. She mouthed a "thank you" as she tucked the swatch in her bag.

"Anyway, Charlotte, I'm crazed. I mean, we're leaving tomorrow on safari and I have nothing, *nothing* to bring as a gift for Ted."

Christ! Another favor, Charlotte muttered to herself.

"So what do you want me to do, Vicky?"

"Make a fast run up Madison," Vicky wheedled. "See what you can find. Pretty, please?"

"No problem," Charlotte replied, grinding her molars. "But just out of curiosity, don't you think bringing Tom is gift enough?'

"I wish," Vicky sighed. "Ted says he's set up all the masseuses in one tent. There's another tent for wardrobe. And he's also sending over his butlers, his personal trainer, a tennis pro, his wife's hairdresser, and the PV…"

"You've lost me there, Vicky. The what?"

"PV. Personal videographer, Charlotte. Where have you been? The guy's been following him around for the past year."

"What the hell for?" Charlotte asked.

"Ted wants a visual memoir of his family. I think it's a marvelous idea."

"Spare me the details, please," Charlotte replied. "I can't imagine anything more boring." "Call me later," Vicky said before hanging up.

An hour later, she was wandering through FM Allen on Madison Avenue. She'd already seen the perfect gift in the window, a 1940s English "cocktail" suitcase. It looked like something Lord Erroll in Happy Valley would have had his porters lug out into the Kenyan bush. *White Mischief* was one of Charlotte's all-time favorite books. The debauchery and deceit, the unutterable boredom, of Britain's upper classes in 1930s colonial Africa, bore an uncanny resemblance to the New York world she now worked in.

The sales clerk lifted the case out of the window and opened it for Charlotte's inspection. Charlotte couldn't believe the case was intact. There were two ebonized trays for lemons, limes, and olives, a miniature glass ice bucket, and six glass decanters with twelve interchangeable silver caps for brandy, bourbon, gin, rye, scotch, rum, wines and fruit juices. Ice tongs, a tiny silver hammer to crush the ice, silver shakers, and linen napkins completed the kit. Charlotte smiled. If there was one thing these Brits had that American billionaires most certainly did not, it was style.

"How much is it?" asked Charlotte.

"$14,000," he answered nonchalantly. "It's going to be in the March issue of *Departures Magazine*."

"Well, if you would, I'd like you to send it up, on approval, to my friend on Park Avenue. I'm sure she'll take it."

"Of course," the man replied, shooting his monogrammed Pinks cuffs. "I'll take it up myself."

The phone was vibrating in her pocket when she walked back into her loft. Slamming the door with her foot, Charlotte flipped it open.

"You're just amazing!" Vicky cooed. "It's the most divine thing I've ever seen. Ted will love it."

"Good! Glad I could help," Charlotte replied, dropping onto the sofa and closing her eyes. Just the sound of Vicky's voice was aggravating. *People only have as much power as you give them. People only have as much power as you give them.* She repeated Anna's phrase to herself like a mantra while rubbing her feet. After Vicky hung up with promises to send a postcard, Charlotte's muscles gradually relaxed. She was reminded, yet again, of the rift that separated the old and newly decadent. Back in Happy Valley, even if they screwed each other's spouses and drank themselves into stupors, they sent thank-you notes in the morning. They had manners.

Dr. Greene had once suggested that Charlotte carried the unresolved issues she had with her mother into her relationship with Vicky, that the two women mirrored one another. Charlotte didn't like how that reflected on herself. For a long time, she'd assumed it was Vicky's marriage that had come between them. Now she knew better...

Like her clients, Vicky liked a life that ran as smooth as honey, no surprises, no bumps. The worst bumps she encountered came at 35,000 feet when she flew on the family's G-5. What was it she'd said to Charlotte when she tried to explain her "need" for the 46-million-dollar aircraft? "There are two things that are important to me, Charlotte: One is avoiding people who might bum me out. And two is protecting my children. Who wants their kids sitting next to some guy who sets his crotch on fire?"

The point was, try and talk to her about real life, about a life that entailed planning ahead, paying a mortgage, taking a taxi, working... Well, you might as well be talking to her about tribal customs in some far-flung region of Kyrgyzstan. Actually, Vicky had been to Kyrgyzstan on a rug buying expedition. Her only decisions seemed to involve choosing between vacations in Anguilla, Lyford or Parrot Cay, wearing Prada or Gucci, and lunching at Swifty's or Bilboquet.

But it was Vicky's stinginess that Charlotte truly resented. Forget the fact that she'd turned down Charlotte's request for a small loan, while she gave millions to charity. Charity was cheap for Vicky. It cost her nothing. It was giving in other ways that had become more complicated. Over the years, Vicky had become suspicious of even the most spontaneous, magnanimous gestures from her friends. Because such gestures carried with them the weight of obligation, of debt. And Vicky didn't like owing anyone anything.

Sometimes, she had wished that their friendship would simply end in a spectacular catfight. Catfights created new beginnings. They cleared the air. Instead, Charlotte had wasted years pussyfooting around minefields of jealousy and envy, never daring to expose or explore her pain. Why did they share only Vicky's joys? Why were her own occasional triumphs tactfully ignored by both of them? And when had the talking, the real talking, stopped? That was what Charlotte missed the most.

Then, she suddenly thought of Anna's shrewd advice over lunch at Boulud. About knowing what to ask for from people. She was right, of course. But part of the delirium, the saving grace of youth, was not knowing. Not caring. *Grabbing the things that glittered*, she thought. Like the gifts that Anna loved. Things that caught the light and dazzled the eye. That was why she had always found it necessary, even easy, to forgive Vicky. Because Vicky had once seemed so utterly dazzling; so much larger than the small, lonely life Charlotte might have led without her.

"The difference between one friend and none is infinity." She'd read that in an Irish novel during her trip to Venice with Paul. Even with Anna as a new friend, Charlotte continued to cling to the habit of hoping that something would change with Vicky. But the pain had grown and hardened inside her like some malignant tumor. When Vicky returned from Botswana, Charlotte would finally end it. She would cut Vicky off and shut her down, just as Vicky had done to her countless times before.

22

The early morning grogginess was troubling. It often signaled the beginning of a bone-deep fatigue. Usually the vividness, that almost painful alertness to sensation, that transformed Charlotte after a killing lasted for weeks. It was exhilarating—the intensity of that awareness. The sun shone brighter. Noises were louder. It even inspired her in her work, gave her a certain clarity of vision. But today, she just felt weary, fed up.

The doctor's appointment at 11:15 loomed over her like some noxious cloud. Cracking her knuckles, she rubbed her eyes. She'd been roaming around Craigslist for hours. She never e-mailed potential "victims" from home. But occasionally, her wanderlust, her need to lose herself online, was so intense, her palms sweated. How would Dr. Greene analyze her obsession with auto parts? Her fascination for postings like: "Got Rhino Grill/Brush. It don't Fit the Ram" or "18 Rims Wit Tires off Escalade" and "For Sale is Hurst Short Shifter?" Sometimes, she liked them so much, she wrote them down. Her other favorite were the Strictly Platonic postings in Personals.

"This Guy's Into Footsmelling" ("I enjoy stockings and socks")

"Female Sasquatch with Bedsores" ("I just want washing and conversation")

"Help! My Hair looks like crap!"

"Dentist Needed Desperately" (I noticed the hole in December. PLEASE—I can't take it anymore.)"

"Tattoo Artist wants to drill you."

"Wrestling Challenge" ("No real violence. Just wanna see who comes out on top. No sex involved.") *No sex, my ass!* Charlotte thought, shutting down her computer and heading off towards the bathroom.

As the needles of hot water worked into the muscles of her back, Charlotte sloughed off the dead skin with a new body wash. It was made of meadow foam oil. Sniffing the bottle, she wondered how exactly one went about collecting meadow foam oil. The product had been a complimentary gift from Rapture, *the* new spa in Soho.

"You're going to love it, Charlotte," one of her clients had promised, after regifting her with a certificate for a morning of free treatments. "It's like a spiritual rebirth."

Greeted on her arrival with a hushed hello from her massage therapist, Charlotte had changed into a pair of fuzzy slippers and a soft linen robe and shuffled along behind her toward the spa's inner sanctum. After four hours in a sepulchral room, breathing in the fragrance of pine-scented incense and trying to block out the sounds of wind chimes, chirping birds, and rolling waves, she still couldn't fathom how this kind of self-indulgence translated into a spiritual "rebirth." What did getting one's skin rubbed, scrubbed, pummeled, exfoliated, detoxed, steamed, wrapped and buffed have to with God?

Toweling off her body, Charlotte applied a thin layer of moisturizer and brushed her wet hair. Pavel had called from Moscow and asked her to pick up a bottle of champagne. She was planning to open the Dom.

"I'm bringing over something very special," he'd said. "Because I think it is an honor to be invited into your home."

"An honor indeed," Charlotte said out loud as she sauntered off naked toward her closet.

23

She was ten minutes late for her doctor's appointment. The room was packed.

"I'm very sorry, Ms. Wolfe," the nurse said when Charlotte checked in at reception. "But the doctor's had an emergency."

"How long is the wait?" Charlotte knew it was a dumb question.

The woman shrugged. "Why don't you sit down, dear, and I'll keep you posted," she said, returning to the ringing phones.

Perched on the edge of a red upholstered chair, Charlotte drummed her fingers on the chrome armrests. As her eyes flickered over the row of vacant faces seated around the room, she realized that there was a bond she shared with these strangers. Like her, they had spent too many years waiting. Waiting for love, for dinner, for subways, for sleep. Waiting for bank loans and dentists, for sex, for success, even for dry cleaning.

Fidgeting restlessly in her chair, Charlotte sighed. W*hoever had said that good things come to those who wait certainly didn't live in New York,* she thought. *Age and death were the only two things that came to those who waited around in this town.* She had been obsessed with death ever since those nights as a child when she'd tried to sing herself to sleep. That was why she'd chosen to block out the pain. To postpone the doctors. She didn't want her fears confirmed. So why had she lied to Anna? Why wasn't she here, making her laugh, quieting her fears? Casting her eyes down when she caught sight of the skeletal features of what had once been a staggeringly beautiful woman, Charlotte struggled against the urge to leave, to jump up and run for the door.

"Most of life is about loss and leaving," Anna had said that night at the Temple Bar. It was the only time she had ever talked about her past; about the loss of her only child and her husband and about sharing her family's country home in Padua with the Nazis during the Second World War.

"I was only eight years old," she'd confided, spearing an olive with her toothpick. "And I sat in the back of a courtroom with my mother while a judge sentenced my father to five years in jail."

"For what? Why?" Charlotte had whispered.

"For collaborating with the enemy," Anna had fumed. "What collaborating? The Germans showed up and took over the house. My father was responsible for his own family and for every farmer on the estate."

Tucking her green silk shirt tightly into her skirt, Anna's words had become rushed. As if by hurrying them, she might distance herself from their meaning, their impact. "When my brother came back from the war, he lost a fortune at the casino in Venice," she had said. "My father, the oldest brother, had to sign for him. For the honor of the family, you know? It was almost medieval then, the north, the Veneto. When my father died three years later in jail, I began to dream of going to America. And here I am," she had added before ordering her third and last martini.

"Lucky for me," Charlotte had replied, giving her a hug.

Anna's jaw dropped.

"I'm drunk," Charlotte had said with a smile. "It won't happen again, I promise."

As the doctor scurried across the room towards his office, Charlotte wondered why Anna's losses hadn't diminished her spirit or her wisdom. "There is nothing lonelier in life than suffering only one's own losses," her friend had murmured to her softly before they parted at the end of that evening. "You should keep that in mind, cara." Quickly picking up her bag and retrieving her coat from the closet near the receptionist, Charlotte headed for the door.

"Miss Wolfe, Miss Wolfe," the woman shouted after her. Charlotte had already disappeared.

24

Stooping down to pick up her newspapers in the elevator, she opened Friday morning's *Post*. The story was the lead on page two.

> **MURDERED MANSION MAMA ROBBED!**
> *Ben Volpone*
>
> One week after the brutal murder of Amy Webb, wife of Wall Street trader Richard Webb, a source close to the investigation reports that police are following up on a number of promising leads. "Although no arrest is imminent, we now know that the perpetrator removed a brown, leather Louis Vuitton vanity case from the premises and that the victim was killed by the same or similar weapon as

that used in other female homicides in Manhattan."

The police source didn't know if the case contained other stolen articles. Meanwhile Mr. Webb, the police and the firm of Goldman Sachs have offered a reward of $50,000 for information leading to the arrest and conviction of the killer. Police ask anyone with information to call (800) 577-TIPS.

Amy Webb, a prominent socialite, was found dead in the dressing room of her home at 32 E. 65th Street. Active in many New York City charities, Webb was also an amateur equestrienne. The funeral service was private.

Charlotte chortled. Some way to be remembered: a socialite and an amateur equestrienne. Then she reread the headline and first paragraph, noting the discrepancy between the words "robbed" and "removed."

She had to assume the police had now made the connection between Craigslist and the killer. But why were they withholding the information from the media? To avoid the possibility of copycats? Had they perhaps posted an ad themselves? Were they monitoring the site? Whatever the reason, Charlotte was still confident that she was safe.

It was remarkable, really, how easy it was to get away with murder. The first time: the woman with the Dom. She hadn't planned it. She'd improvised. The memories of Charlotte's missions were always fragmented, splintered into shards of sensation. The vision of the woman at the door, for instance. She was shrieking. "The fucking bastard. Thinks he's cutting me off with $70,000 a month." Dressed in skintight jeans, a skimpy wifebeater, and four-inch cork platform shoes, she looked like she was dying of Chronic Wasting Disease.

"So did you bring cash?" she'd asked greedily, while pulling out a gold compact.

Charlotte had nodded, mute with distaste.

Then there was the photograph of the woman's young daughter in the living room. No older than twelve or thirteen, the kid was dressed in the same $400 sprayed-on jeans and wifebeater as her mother. But her eyes, rimmed in thick black kohl, already had the spirit sucked right out of them. Her feeble attempt to match her mother's smile seemed almost grotesque. Charlotte recognized herself in that smile. She felt as if she should look away, as if it was indecent, seeing the girl's pain.

She had imagined the insane rush of adolescent hormones, the pole-vaulting leaps between euphoria, doubt, and despair. How she'd loathed those inconsolably lonely years as a teenager. "Do me a favor, dear. Don't even look at her!" the woman spat out, dumping a silver tray on the driftwood coffee table and pouring herself a tumbler of champagne. "The two of us were tighter than my jeans," she said, slapping her own butt. "But she chose to live with her father, if you can believe it. Just up and deserted me. Not even a note. I found out from the lawyers."

Charlotte's head had buzzed. She could still almost feel the heat of adrenaline. When the woman belched and rose unsteadily to her feet, Charlotte had reached around behind her, searching, blindly, for the poker next to the fireplace. It was the third fire tool in. She'd counted.

Keep her talking, keep her talking, a voice inside had

prompted her. "It must be hard, being here alone," she said to the woman. "I mean, without your daughter or your husband."

"Him! I'd like to kill him," the woman whispered. "Like that woman in Hong Kong who served her husband a nice, cyanide-laced, chocolate milkshake." As Charlotte's fingers found a grip on the poker, the tumbler of champagne slid out of the woman's hand.

"Shit!" she'd said, leaning over to pick it up from the carpet. Which is when Charlotte swung the poker up from behind her and clubbed her on the head.

The woman slumped down and gurgled. Blood had spattered across the carpet and the driftwood table. Her skinny martini-legs were doing this weird butterfly kick. And her head was all wobbly. Bending her knees and driving the poker straight down into the crown of the woman's skull, Charlotte suddenly thought of her nanny pointing out the soft spot on her sister's head when she first came home from the hospital. And just like that, it was over.

There had only been a tiny splotch of blood on Charlotte's jeans. After rolling up the poker in her yoga mat, she'd grabbed a bottle of Dom from the vestibule, buttoned up her slicker, and walked down the fire stairs to the garage in the basement. From then on, the poker had become a talisman, the instrument of Charlotte's transformation. Like the banners beneath which medieval knights would rally their forces before galloping into battle, it was an extension of herself: straight, strong and true to its purpose.

Climbing reluctantly out of her bed, she pulled back the heavy damask curtains, put on a pair of red wooly socks, and walked towards the kitchen. *Pavel was probably somewhere over Newfoundland by now,* she thought. He'd left a message on her cell, promising to be there at six. She was as nervous as a teenager. What would she wear? Something casual but sexy. Maybe the black silk harem pants and a plain white t-shirt. *Perfect,* she thought. And a pair of old red sequined Converse. She'd devote the rest of the day to pulling together her vision of the dacha. Laying out swipes from magazines, the color palette, her swatches and sketches ... This was probably the only step left in the process of decorating that she still looked forward to. *Like dreaming out loud,* she whispered, picking up the tarnished silver framed photo of her Aunt Dottie before heading off to polish it.

25

When Charlotte saw Pavel stabbing at the fire with the poker, she almost dropped the toast points.

"Russians are good with fire, Charlotte," he said with a grin. "And this one needs help."

She smiled. "I'm pretty good with a poker, too, Pavel. You'd be surprised."

"Perhaps," he said, coaxing a shower of sparks from a log. "But I enjoy this. I do not have time anymore for such ordinary jobs."

Setting down the platter of toast on her Indian coffee table, she giggled.

"What is it?" Pavel asked, putting the poker back in its place. "What is funny?"

"There's enough Beluga here for the whole block. And I

can't believe you brought $4,000 worth of caviar over in a Tupperware bowl. There's something absurd about it."

"No more absurd than a once-poor Jew like me eating it," he said, almost wistfully. "My mother loves Tupperware."

"I'm sorry, Pavel. Really. Why don't you open the Dom?"

As he prowled around the near the windows, his hands clenched into fists, the room seemed to bristle with repressed energy. *Like a giant in a dollhouse*, Charlotte thought to herself as she eyed him, warily, from the couch.

"I am sorry, Charlotte. You see, I have just opened my new hotel."

"But that's great news, Pavel," Charlotte said. "Congratulations! We should toast your new success!"

Suddenly, his fist hit the wall and Charlotte shrank into her chair.

"It is a disaster, Charlotte. It nearly killed me. Getting the money, finding the workers, and now..."

"What? Nobody came?" Charlotte asked. "You have no guests?"

"Oh! I have guests," Pavel retorted, licking his fist, as the cork flew across the room. "They steal everything. They steal the pillows, the sheets, the paintings on the walls."

"We call it pilfering, Pavel. It's a problem in hotels here, too."

Pavel grinned. "You call it pilfering when guests check out, carrying off a six-foot gold mirror in my lobby? In front of my people at reception?"

Charlotte tried to imagine a similar scene taking place in the lobby of the Carlyle. "That's unbelievable," she said. "Why didn't they call the police or try to stop them?"

"The police are criminals, too, Charlotte. So now my hotel is like a prison. I have bolted the beds and chairs to the floor. I have removed all the rugs and the decorations. It's..."

"A catastrophe?" Charlotte offered, touching his sleeve. *Did this man ever sit down?* She wondered.

"No. It's business as usual in Russia, Charlotte. This is what freedom means to us now. Permission to steal just a little bit more. But let's drink," he said, filling her glass.

Charlotte smiled as Pavel passed her the crystal flute of champagne and a toast point with so much caviar on it, she had to cup her hand under her chin to catch the eggs.

"You are still smiling, Charlotte. Is it the Tupperware?"

"No. I was thinking of you and the burning building," she replied.

Pavel laughed. "The night I break my window and crawl out? When the firemen are all standing around smoking cigarettes?"

"Yes," Charlotte said, as she crunched her toast and the first mouthful of pearl-like eggs slid down her throat. "You yelled at them. 'Why for God's sake don't you come in and get me?'"

"We ring your bell and nobody answered," Pavel said, finishing the story as he attempted to squeeze his 6' 4" frame into the confines of a velvet slipper chair. "I am choking on smoke and they wait for me to answer my doorbell."

"Pavel, come over here," Charlotte said, indicating a place for him on the sofa. "It's making me uncomfortable, just watching you."

"Here's to your beauty," he said, touching her glass and sitting down next to her.

"Would you like to hear some more Russian stories?" he asked, taking a slow sip of the Dom.

"You mean fairytales, Pavel?" she replied, pulling her knees up in front of the fire. "I would love to."

"We Russians have always believed in fairytales, Charlotte," Pavel said. "Because in our country, they come true."

Was he being facetious? God knows, the news from Russia was like something straight out of Grimms: gassing theaters, killing schoolchildren, murders and mobsters. There were questions, however, that Charlotte simply didn't ask Pavel. How he really made his money. Why it was safer for his family to live in New Jersey than Moscow.

"Let me give you one example of a Russian fairytale, OK?" he suggested, leaning over and stirring the champagne bubbles in her glass. "It is a true story." Scooping up a spoonful of caviar, he swallowed and began to speak.

"One weekend last winter, I go cross-country skiing. It is perfect for this, the area around my dacha. I am gone for hours before I realize I am lost. And it is getting dark. Snow is falling, faster and faster. Then I hear these bells. The sound is, how you say, muffled by the snow? I follow the sound. And there in the middle of the forest is a village with a brand new church. This village is still full of old wooden houses, *izbahs*, we call them. Like gingerbread houses in old books. Except for the church, life is just as it was two centuries ago. There are women lined up at the well, helping each other put pails of water on wooden … on wooden…"

"Poles," Charlotte whispered. "I think you mean poles." She felt as if she'd been cast under a spell; touched in a way that made even her toes tingle. She wasn't sure she liked it.

"Are you OK?" Pavel asked, brushing his fingers against her knees.

"Yes, I'm fine," Charlotte replied. "Don't stop."

"So the men take me into a home and feed me by candlelight," Pavel said, quietly resuming his story. "We drink vodka and talk about the church. Then they introduce me to this ninety-five-year-old woman. She saw the church in a dream, Charlotte. The dream went on for weeks. And she understood this was a message. So for three years, she took the train into Moscow every day, all alone, and begged for money to build it. One old poor woman, Charlotte, a widow from the forest made a dream come true. And thanks to her dream, I am saved by the bell! I found my way home. This is ironic, no? And a good fairytale?"

Charlotte had been so entranced, she'd drunk three glasses of Dom. Her head was spinning.

"Charlotte?" Pavel said, touching her knee again.

She blinked.

"Aha!" laughed Pavel. "You have surrendered to what we Russians call *shamanstvo*. It is like an enchantment."

"I guess so. I mean, yes!" she said, hardly daring to look him in the eye. "I'm not used to drinking so much."

Pavel chuckled. "Charlotte, how lucky you are. For us, this Dom is like sipping teardrops."

"You're a poet, Pavel."

"No, Charlotte," Pavel said, with a grimace as he sat suddenly rigid in his chair. "I am most definitely not a poet. There is a dark side to our fairytales, too."

"I know. I've read..." Charlotte said, gently placing her glass on the table and glancing over at him.

Pavel shook his head. "I am not speaking of those nightmares that make it onto your televisions here, Charlotte."

"So tell me, Pavel." Charlotte said, gazing intently at his face. "Please."

"In the village where I have my dacha, I am like a god. The peasants—and yes, we still call them peasants—love me and fear me. This terror and love is just as it was with the czars and the priests and the communists. They see me arrive in my black Mercedes and hear about my indoor swimming pool and my eight bathrooms. It makes them angry."

"Well, of course, it makes them angry," said Charlotte.

"It makes them so angry, they kill for a handful of rubles. Perhaps, not in my village, not yet, but in Moscow where poor men know that the rich are also killing for billions of American dollars."

"Oligarchs, you mean?" Charlotte said, thinking of the *Vanity Fair* article she'd read about the guy who owned a yacht with its own submarine.

"Oligarchs, yes," Pavel confirmed, with a wave of his hand. "And many others, too. The point is, the poor man and the rich man in Russia today are the same, Charlotte. They share the same rage, the same dead eyes, the same hunger. The rich men shop like the starving eat. The shopping is new for us. The killing is not. But we do both with a vengeance, believe me."

"It's not so different here, Pavel," Charlotte added, eagerly. "The rich and the poor, the hostility. "

"It is *not* the same, Charlotte. Can you imagine your government dumping radioactive waste in the middle of New York City? This happened in Moscow. Or going to the market and buying a lovely fat watermelon for your family? Then finding out that it came from the Zone of Exclusion near Chernobyl? No, Charlotte. You know nothing of a Russian's rage; of our monsters or the bloody, savage birth of hope at a time when even the earth itself is dying."

Charlotte sat there, her mouth open. "I'm sorry. I had no idea," she said, contritely.

"And now I must go. My wife and children are waiting."

Charlotte usually preferred to be first at the door, to preempt other people's departures. But tonight, she followed meekly after Pavel.

"We have to talk about work," she said, pointing towards the sketches and swatches that she'd laid out near the fireplace. Pulling on his coat, Pavel grinned. "Of course. That is why I am here … to talk about furniture."

"If you are here Monday during the day, I would like to take you up to meet Max," Charlotte said, pulling out a leather book. "He has a shop I think you'll love."

"I am yours. But only if you promise to have dinner with me before I go back to Moscow? Will you do that, Charlotte?" Charlotte pretended to check her book.

"I think I'm free on Tuesday night."

"Then Tuesday it is," Pavel said, giving her a gentle peck on the cheek.

Charlotte accompanied him to the elevator and, as the doors began to close, leapt into the gap. "Wait!" She shouted, sliding up against the wall inside. "I'll take you down." The two shared an easy, companionable silence all the way to the lobby. It was only when Charlotte stood beneath the awning, gawking at the bodyguards that she spoke. "They're as big as armoires, those guys," she said.

Pavel flinched. "A necessary evil," he replied, as one of the men opened the door to the limo and Pavel lowered his head to get in.

"See you Monday," he said, disappearing into the darkness.

Riding up in the elevator, Charlotte wondered if Pavel had been referring to himself in his story. Was he one of the rich men who killed for billions of dollars? Had she found a kindred soul? A man who would understand the extraordinary thing that made her so different from others? Money hadn't yet thinned Pavel's blood. There was something that felt so fresh about his struggle. So raw.

Sipping a final glass of Dom and making room for the Tupperware bowl in her fridge, Charlotte thought about the old lady and her dream of the church. It reminded her of her own recurrent dream. Was the dream about being chased by her mother a premonition, a message? Scrubbing her hands in soapy water, she touched the old marble sink, as if to reassure herself. And as she had done so many times before, Charlotte wondered what it might have been like to have had a sister in her life.

After giving her hair its usual one hundred slow luxurious strokes, she slipped into Vicky's old cashmere and touched the silver framed photo next to her bed. Sometimes, she'd find herself speaking to Aunt Dottie, hoping that she was alive somewhere, listening. *Was it worth the price that her mother had paid, losing an entire family?* she wondered. For what? For party invitations? For an apartment on Fifth Avenue and a membership at the Cosmo Club?

Charlotte closed her eyes and slept like the dead.

26

Charlotte was admiring the work her French painters had done in Rita's foyer (twelve coats of a lovely two-tone gray lacquer) when her client stormed in the front door. She was wearing a brace on her right wrist.

"My God!" Charlotte said. "What happened?"

"Don't ask. Don't even ask!" Rita said, making a clumsy effort to remove a black kid glove from her left hand.

"I'm asking anyway," Charlotte said, leaning down to help remove the glove.

"You won't believe it," Rita added. "But yesterday I went to the orthopedist. I've had these horrible pains in my wrist, Charlotte, for weeks."

"It sounds like carpal tunnel," Charlotte said, feigning sympathy.

"So the doctor says to me: 'Mrs. Brickman, you're the third woman in here this month with the same complaint.' I'm kneading my arm, anything to get rid of the pain, Charlotte. And then he says: 'Do you, by any chance, own a Birkin bag?' 'Of course, I own a Birkin bag,' I said to him. 'It was a present from my husband.' So, he says to me, 'Well, it's BBS, Mrs. Brickman, Birkin Bag Syndrome. Carrying all that the weight in the crook of your arm has damaged your nerves.

You'll have to put the bag away and wear a brace.'"

"Do you have any idea how long I waited for that Birkin?" Rita fumed. "I'm going to sue Hermes!"

Hers, of course, was *no ordinary* Birkin. Charlotte recalled the gloating phone call from Rita, a year earlier. Abe had somehow gotten his hands on one of six $78,000 anniversary Birkins with diamonds in the locket. He'd flown an assistant all the way to Honolulu to pick it up. Watching silently while Rita handed her new sable coat over to one of the maids, Charlotte noticed that a few stray hairs had managed to work themselves loose from her tight little updo. And there was a button missing from her cashmere cardigan. Neither was a good sign.

Wasting no time on further niceties, Rita launched herself into the next scathing tirade.

"And as if my life isn't complicated enough, Charlotte ... my daughter, my adorable ten-year-old daughter, has lice!"

Charlotte simply raised an eyebrow in response. Rita hated being interrupted during her tirades.

"We are paying $35,000 a year plus thousands more in donations to the fanciest private girls' school in New York, and she has lice. I mean, what kind of children are they taking in over there?"

"I have no idea, Rita," Charlotte said, picking at her cuticles.

"So I get myself over to the Whiting School, Charlotte, after forcing that feckless headmaster, Robinson, to talk to me. And do you know what he says to me? To *me*, one of the biggest contributors to their annual fund?"

More rhetorical questions, thought Charlotte.

"He says, 'Rita, you should hire a professional nitpicker.'"

"What's a nitpicker?" Charlotte asked, fighting off a fit of giggles, and carefully moving toward a chair in the living room.

"It's a person who charges $100 an hour, Charlotte, to comb through my child's lice-ridden hair like one of those grooming monkeys, on a Channel 13 documentary!"

Rita collapsed on a chair. "I need something to drink, Charlotte. Please, get me some water or juice. I'm exhausted."

Charlotte reached for the small, embroidered, crewelwork pouch on the coffee table. The words "Ring My Bell" were stitched on the outside of the pouch in yellow thread. The pouch concealed a small wireless device used to summon the help. Similar pouches were scattered casually all over the house. Charlotte pressed the unseen button and wondered, yet again, if the embroidered words were supposed to be funny.

"Lice are rather common these days, Rita," she said, fanning her fire. "So are bedbugs."

"Bedbugs!?" Rita's wail brought the young Ecuadorian girl, the one Charlotte had last seen at the Vineyard, scurrying into the room.

"Yes, I read somewhere that there's an epidemic of bedbugs in the city."

Ignoring the detour on bedbugs, Rita continued haranguing Charlotte as the maid stood there, waiting for her orders.

"Rita, didn't you say you wanted something to drink?"

"Oh! Yes," Rita hurumphed, turning to look at the girl. "Alba, bring me some ap-ple juice. Ap-ple. And I want the ice cubes made from Fiji water. Comprende?"

"Si, Senora. Right away."

Charlotte was in such a buoyant mood after seeing Pavel, it didn't even annoy her that Rita hadn't bothered to ask her if she, too, might enjoy a drink.

"Listen, Rita," Charlotte said, sweetly. "I'd love to hear more about all this, but you said it was important I make time for you today."

"You're right, Charlotte," Rita said, giving a tug to her Carolina Herrera skirt and standing up. "If you just give me one minute. I have something to show you."

As Charlotte sipped Rita's apple juice, a young man slipped into the living room and began knife-creasing, plumping, and rearranging the down pillows. Rita was one of many clients who hired a professional pillow person to come in once a week. *How ludicrous*, Charlotte thought. While the rest of the world worried about terrorists, tsunamis, wars, and deadly viruses, Rita worried about her pillows, lice, and nitpickers.

Bored and impatient, Charlotte skimmed through the titles of Rita's newest "must reads" stacked on a Hepplewhite side table. *The Angry Self, The Dance of Anger, Angry Kids, Anger Busting 101.* The truth was, Rita probably spent three hours a week talking to her shrink about feeling angry. When she wasn't talking about it or just plain feeling it, she was reading about feeling it. *What a vicious circle*, she chuckled.

Charlotte picked up a glossy brochure. The shiny retro blue and white plaid cover featured a cute vintage logo with the word "COOKBOOK" floating in the center. When she saw the words "Whiting School Annual Report" printed beneath it, Charlotte snorted a laugh.

Had they never heard the expression "cooking the books?" she thought.

"Pretty funny, huh? Charlotte?" The unexpected sound of Abe's deep, throaty voice startled her. The brochure dropped to the floor. "It's okay. I laughed, too," said Abe, as he came around her to shake hands.

"I guess they have a great sense of humor," Charlotte said.

"No, Charlotte. The problem is, they have *no* sense of humor," Abe replied. "Why do you suppose the world has become so tediously earnest? And you don't have to answer that."

Charlotte liked Abe. Bald, chunky, and dressed in a pair of beat-up old jeans and running shoes, he was delightfully unpretentious. Charlotte's relationships with the husbands of her clients played a pivotal part in her success. After years watching her mother manipulate rich, powerful men, she had learned how to please them. Accustomed to subservience, she knew that they also enjoyed the occasional challenge—a woman who, far from appearing to be intimidated, came in close enough to puncture their thick skins; to make them laugh at themselves. Charlotte felt there was nothing more seductive in a woman than this ability to make a man laugh at himself.

Today, she watched him as he struggled for something to say. It touched her that he chose to make that effort.

"Are you here to talk about moving the pool?" he asked with a small smile.

"I sincerely hope not," Charlotte answered, honestly.

"Good! It's the Johnsons, you know. My wife wants them to put us up for membership at the Ocean Club. She thinks that moving the pool will, somehow, increase our chances."

"I see," she replied, wondering what Abe thought of Birkin Bag Syndrome.

"Ah! Here she is," Abe said, hurrying over to give his wife a kiss.

Rita was carrying a large manila envelope. "I hope the wrist feels a bit better, dear?"

"Don't mention it, please, Abe," Rita said. "I was just going to show Charlotte the paint chips for the new house on Dyer's Lane."

"*What* new house on Dyer's Lane?" Charlotte felt as if she'd been ambushed.

"Well, I'll leave you to it," Abe said, sensing the possibility of an unpleasant scene.

"We've bought another little place on the Vineyard, Charlotte," Rita said, "on Lake Tashmoo."

"What for, Rita? The place in Gay Head is so beautiful."

"Yes, but it's on the ocean. I like the idea of having a place on a lake, too. It's so much more tranquil. I'm going to use it to meditate," Rita added, opening the manila envelope and spilling a pile of paint chips onto a $100,000 Chinese rug that Charlotte had finally found at auction in London.

"Talk to me, Rita, please talk to me," Charlotte said, trying to remain absolutely calm.

"Don't get upset, Charlotte. I know how busy you've been. So I decided to just go ahead and hire a professional colorist."

"Rita, this is nothing but white paint," she said, forcing herself to smile while rifling through the pile.

"It's thirty-two different shades of white paint, Charlotte. The colorist thinks that the shade has to be exactly right. Because of the light, you see? The light up there changes all the time."

"You're not Picasso or de Kooning, Rita. What do you care about the changes in light?"

Charlotte could see that Rita was annoyed. Her nose was twitching. "Just take these home with you, Charlotte. And call me when you've calmed down, alright?"

"Fine, no problem," said Charlotte, gathering up her coat and gloves from the chair.

"We're not doing any work on the place till the spring. So you have plenty of time," Rita said, bussing her on the left cheek. "It's going to be great fun, I promise."

Charlotte snatched the paint chips and shoved them into the side of her bag before slowly walking out of the apartment. She took careful, measured steps, like a drunk pretending to be sober. The only thing that improved her mood was the text message from Pavel. "Thank you, Charlotte, for such a wonderful New York evening. I will call you later about dinner on Tuesday and the visit to Max." That and the fact Rita hadn't even mentioned moving the pool.

27

Sunday morning was blissful. She'd taken a three mile speedwalk up from Battery Park to the piers before breakfast. Stopping to stretch and drink a cappuccino, she stood beneath the rusted, old White Star Liner gates on 14th Street. This was where the Titanic had been scheduled to arrive before it hit the iceberg. Charlotte was not a traveler, not in the real sense of the word, but twice a year, she flew the same migratory route as the rich and restless nomads she so religiously served: Paris, London, St. Barth's, Rome,

Aspen. Last year, she'd even been to Morocco and the year before, to Rajasthan.

Charlotte's travel was like reading Page 6 in the *Post*. It gave her something to talk about with clients. It made them feel more comfortable, imagining that their decorator shared the same "taste" in travel. It was like sharing her visits with her shrink. The shrink proved that Charlotte wasn't perfect. It made her clients feel less inadequate. But Pavel and his fairytales, the story of the dacha, the silent, snow-filled forests, and even Moscow, had spurred a sudden longing to get away. Far away. And to go by sea on a private yacht. To be surrounded by nothing but water and sky. To be unmoored...

A gust of freezing wind tossed bits of litter into the air as Charlotte turned around to jog back home. She'd take her time reading the papers and look at the "brand" profile that had been e-mailed to her from Darryl's handlers. Their letter explained that it was important for Darryl's home—and therefore Charlotte's work—to reflect Darryl's overall brand image. "Handlers!" Charlotte sneered. *What a perfect word*, she thought. After all, it is what they call people who train circus animals.

As she turned the corner onto North Moore Street, she noticed a white van parked in front of her building. "Nothing dull here!" read the sign on the side of the van. The license plate read: BSHARP. It was Leo. Every year, he drove up from Florida and circled the neighborhood, stopping to sharpen kitchen knives and garden tools.

"Hey, Leo. It's me, Charlotte!" she said, running up to shake hands with the wizened old white man leaning up against the van. His skin was as brown and wrinkled as an alligator.

"How's business?" she asked.

"Not bad." Leo replied, nodding towards the bright red SUV parked behind him. "These are all his," he added, holding up a bouquet of lethal-looking silver scissors.

A very large bald black man sat inside the SUV, pounding on the steering wheel. The throaty bass from his woofers shook the vehicle. The word "BREATHE" was written in white script across his windshield. The letters were so big, Charlotte couldn't imagine how the guy could even see the road. Splinters of sunlight reflected off the floating gold "rims" or "dubs" as Charlotte now called hub caps after her midnight rambles through the Auto Parts section of the List. Charlotte breathed. Deeply.

"I'll bring you some coffee in an hour or so, Leo," she said, fleeing inside the building.

An hour later, she was lying on the couch and skimming through "The Hunt," her favorite new column in the *New York Times* Real Estate Section. These stories about poor, struggling yuppies, students launching careers, and middle-class families searching for somewhere to lay their heads in Manhattan always made Charlotte feel richer. The funniest piece this week was in the Metro section. Some architect had cut a hole in the wall above a bedroom door and stuffed a mattress in it. It was supposed to be a joke. When he posted an ad on Craigslist for "an elevated, mattress-sized space between rooms," he got over a dozen requests to rent it.

Charlotte had drunk too many cups of coffee. Her hands

were jittery. Squeezing her eyes shut, she massaged her temples. Silvery spears of light flickered as a series of wildly dissonant, dizzying images sped through the darkness. First she saw the trustees' dinner at the museum, the Brickmans' fifteen-room duplex, their two houses at the Vineyard, and Rita's $78,000 Birkin bag. Then she caught a glimpse of the women in that Russian village, still hauling pails of water around on wooden poles; of Amy Webb's mansion and $350 silk underpants. Opening her eyes, she remembered Vicky's $14,000 cocktail suitcase and Darryl's 12,000-square-foot apartment. Finally, she thought about John, the homeless man, commuting to a street corner from his shelter every day, and the hulking black man pounding on his steering wheel while he waited for his scissors.

For more than thirty years, Charlotte had gone out of her way to avoid thinking. Thinking implied that something might be thawing inside, like the tingling that she'd felt in her toes when Pavel was talking. Thinking triggered questions and doubts. Charlotte couldn't afford the luxury of either. Pavel had been furious on Friday night when she had implied that there might be similarities between life in Russia and New York.

There were similarities. It wasn't just the chasm that separated the unimaginably rich from everyone else; "the haves from the have yachts" as Vicky snidely put it. It was the murderous, suffocating rage that had inspired the black guy to write the word "BREATHE" on his windshield. Nobody could breathe anymore.

Last summer, she'd had to deal with this one woman who literally couldn't breathe; who was so allergic, so "sensitive," to everything on the face of the earth, Charlotte had to hire an environmental consultant just to choose the freakin' fabrics. Then she'd brought in an acoustician, too. The woman was so "sensitive" to noise, she insisted that the sound of slamming car doors, fourteen floors below on Park Avenue, was giving her migraines. Lowering the ceilings and installing duct work for the air-conditioning system had been another nightmare. "I don't want any insulation, no fibers, nothing that might get into my lungs!" the woman had shouted. When she'd also demanded that they find a way to pump pure oxygen into the apartment, it was the engineer who'd finally shut her up. "You wanna blow this whole fuckin' dump sky-high, lady? Go ahead and put in your oxygen."

Tom, the masseuse, had a theory that the allergies were part of what made these women feel special—that they were fragile and needed to be handled with as much care as their precious antique furnishings. Charlotte suspected that the allergies were just another symptom of rage. "Rage isn't an emotion," her shrink had once claimed. "It's an attempt to hide from emotion. To avoid sadness issues." Charlotte herself had no time for sadness. Sadness was for the weak. For "victims" who blamed everyone but themselves for their unhappiness.

But in July, an old client had told her about a visit to the shrine of some Sufi saint in Iran. "Please do not worry yourself," the guide had gently warned her client before ushering her towards the silent chamber. "Everyone who enters this room cries." Her client had laughed until she sat down on the bare stone floor, closed her eyes, and began to sob, uncontrollably. "It was the strangest sensation," she'd said to Charlotte wistfully. "Like being embraced by this aura of absolute goodness. I couldn't help myself."

At the time, Charlotte had thought that the shrine should have a patent pending. No more anger management, Buddhism, Botox, panic rooms, antidepressants, compulsive shopping or painkillers. Just a shrine set aside for her clients to sob or better yet, to laugh.

Flinging the *Times* and her new client's "brand" identity file on the counter, Charlotte got up to get dressed. There was a new Kinko's down on Trinity Place. She'd go and do some browsing.

28

After a brief breakfast talk with Anna, (who was leaving for Italy to stay with her sister for three weeks) Charlotte spent the rest of Monday morning catching up on invoices. Getting money out of Darryl was so deviously complicated, it was practically Byzantine. She was billing some hotel down in Uruguay for work she was doing on their apartment in New York. The hotel was a tax shelter. Darryl's husband had tried to explain how the system worked. A lot of rich people were doing it, but Charlotte had no interest in understanding how the system worked or even if it was legal. She just wanted to be paid.

Last night at Kinko's had been interesting. She'd found another potential candidate in Collectibles—a woman selling 12 sterling silver Tiffany place settings. Scrolling down to the posting, she'd clicked, and there it was. In red ink, next to the flagged warning about scams and fraud:

> We are aware of the unconfirmed rumors, we repeat, unconfirmed rumors, about a tenuous connection between the Internet and recent homicides in New York City. We recommend that users in New York exercise the usual caution and common sense when dealing with unknown buyers and sellers. If you have any information that might pertain to the unfortunate, tragic events in New York, contact the Craigslist Abuse Team at abuse@Craigslist.org or call the NYPD at 1-800-TIP-LINE.

Twisting the emerald ring that Paul had given her in Venice ("Let's go for the gold," he'd said with a promising smile as they sipped Camparis on the terrace of the Gritti Palace), Charlotte's own caution and common sense had led her to the decision to lay low. But there wasn't any harm in just e-mailing the woman, was there?

29

On Monday afternoon, Charlotte speedwalked from home up to the Carlyle Hotel on Madison Avenue. Standing alone in the living room with its $85,000 a month view over Central Park, Charlotte glanced at Darryl's new elliptical machine. It stood there like some gigantic metal insect, waiting to paralyze its prey. For Charlotte, the elliptical machine was to exercise what puggles were to dogs. Stupid, unnecessary, and phenomenally popular among those who were terminally bored and in constant search of novelty.

Longing to cover or remove the eyesore from the room, Charlotte realized that every minute, every hour, of Darryl's life was scheduled. She lived like a soldier: the regimen, the discipline, the grueling workouts. But the only thing she was fighting for was her sanity. There was no pleasure in it. No passion. It was just another way of killing time.

Speaking of which… Darryl had called at six in the morning and asked her to return the photos to the gallery in Chelsea.

"Listen, I really am sorry," she'd said while Charlotte stared, bleary eyed at her digital clock. "But some little brat came over for a playdate with the kids and tattletaled to his parents. The mommy called and said the nudity on our walls was 'age inappropriate.'"

"No problem," Charlotte had muttered, desperate to go back to sleep. "But what in God's name are you doing up at six o'clock, Darryl?"

"Working out!" she replied huskily. My trainer's leaving for L.A. and this was the only time he could squeeze me in."

"Well, that's just great, Darryl but I'm still sleeping," Charlotte said as she began to burrow her head beneath the pillows.

"Charlotte, wait!" Darryl had hollered as Charlotte's finger was poised on the End Call button. "I need to thank you for something else, too."

"For what?"

"For the fact that my husband is actually sleeping with me again."

"Sorry, Darryl. I…" Being forced to listen to the intimate down and dirty details of her clients' private lives always made Charlotte squirm.

"It's the bed, Charlotte. He loves the bed…"

"Ohhh! Right. Did the guys deliver it?"

"Last night. And I'm still sore!"

Charlotte laughed weakly. "Well, then I guess it was a small price to pay, huh?" she said.

Darryl giggled. "You're too much, Charlotte. I adore you!"

Bubble wrapping the photos of the naked couples, Charlotte thought about the "small price" that Darryl had paid for the pleasures of her new bed. It was just under $200,000. The $70,000 mattress had been custom-made by Hästens, the Swedish mattress makers that supplied beds to that country's royal family. And the frame, a miracle of modern industrial design, had come in at around $130,000.

It wasn't just any frame, of course. An architect friend of Charlotte's had done the drawings and created a plasticene model of the bed, which had then been scanned by a computer imaging wand. After approvals, CAD/CAM had laser-carved a life-size model of the king-size bed in Styrofoam, which was delivered to a Brooklyn workshop. There, a team of Irish millworkers had spent three months handcarving the actual bed from teak, matching their work to every sensuous curve and detail of the model. The project had taken a little over five months from start to Darryl's orgasmic finish.

After carting the package downstairs, she waited while a doorman hailed her a cab. As she buckled herself into the back seat of the taxi, she skimmed through the list of loot in Jerry's swag bag. How many celebs actually needed a twenty-four-karat gold Shu Uemura eyelash curler, a Tupperware ice cream scooper, and—Charlotte especially loved this—one year's worth of free burritos from Chipotle? The list also included a Fendi silk shawl, a three-month bi-coastal membership to the Sports Club LA (with branches in all major cities, of course), a three-month Vespa rental, and $2,000 towards LASIK vision correction. $15 to $25 million dollars a picture wasn't enough for these guys? They had to have swag bags, too? *Always un poquito mas! A little more. That was their motto!*

Charlotte crumpled the embossed paper into a ball, and threw it on the floor. *Breathe, Charlotte! Breathe!* she said to herself, opening the cab window and feeling the slap of cold wind on her cheeks. God! How she hoped Pavel would like the piece at Max's. It was her first major purchase for the dacha. She didn't want to disappoint him.

30

When her cab pulled up and let her out in front of the shop, she nodded at Pavel's two bodyguards and quietly pulled open the door. Huddled in the shadows at the front, she watched as Max rubbed the top of an oak chest the way you rub a kid's stomach when it hurts. Around and around went the hand as he talked.

"Ya gotta pick out the merits of every single piece, Pavel. Somebody asks me, 'What's the best piece here?' Well, that's like askin' the mother of eight children to pick her favorite. There's somethin' good, even in a bad piece. It's like bein' human, ya know?"

Standing perfectly still, she waited to hear where else he might be headed with his conversation.

"See, I want a lunatic like me here in my store. Somebody who feels and sees the character of a piece. That's where the real value is. It's got nothing to do with price."

The hell it doesn't, Charlotte thought to herself, reminded of the $550,000 they'd settled on for the cassa panca.

"It's an instinct. What I hope for is what I call the depth charge feeling, Pavel."

"Sorry, Max," Pavel interrupted. "But depth charge?"

"Yeah! Ya get to a certain point down at 800 feet in the ocean and bang!" Max pounded on the chest. "Ya don't know when it will happen. But you live with a piece long enough and ya get up one night cause ya can't sleep, and it hits you. Ya see it. Ya feel it."

"Hey, Charlotte," Max shouted. "I know you're there. I see ya. I feel ya."

Stepping out from the shadows, Charlotte saw Max giving her his impish grin. "Hello, Charlotte. Ready for my tour?" he asked, bouncing on his toes.

Leading them like elves into the gloom, Max switched on an overhead pin spot and stood next to the cassa panca chest. The colors were even brighter than Charlotte remembered. And the men depicted on the bench, in their velvets and beards, looked almost *alive*. Their eyes seemed to follow

Charlotte's every move. She held her breath as Max began to weave his magical tale about its history.

Pavel was entranced. His hands ran over each figure, touching the folds in the velvet.

"Maybe I am lunatic, Max," Pavel finally said. "But I believe this piece has character. I feel the depth charge!"

"With what you're paying, mister," Max said in a deadpan tone, "you better feel the depth charge!"

She could hear the men laughing as she finally meandered up front. When Pavel reached out and took her hand, she trembled. He looked at her before letting go. "You are shaking, Charlotte. I feel it."

"It's the cold," she answered. "I'm thin-skinned."

"I'm being too forward, perhaps? I'm sorry."

Charlotte noticed Max eyeing their exchange.

"No!" she replied, quietly grabbing his hand. It wasn't the fact that he'd taken her hand, but the warmth of his touch that had made her tremble. Holding hands was such a simple, human gesture. She saw people do it all the time. But she had no memory of anyone ever holding hers. Not even her nanny. The intimacy of the gesture took her breath away. As they walked toward the door, Max picked up the phone. She was certain he was calling Anna. It was almost tribal, the way news traveled in the trade.

"Would you like a ride, Charlotte?" Pavel offered, hopefully, as they closed the door behind them.

"Sure," said Charlotte. "I have a lot of work but maybe you could drop me off somewhere in midtown."

"Of course, it would be my pleasure," Pavel said, inviting her to slide into the limo. "I owe you. Not just for the piece, but the chance to meet such an extraordinary man."

"What were you two talking about, anyway?" Charlotte asked, leaning back against the luxuriously soft leather seat.

"Max's grandfather was a tailor up in the Bronx," Pavel said, now keeping a polite distance between them. "He said that his mother covered all the furniture in plastic. That's why he ended up loving a nice patiner."

"Patin*a*," Charlotte gently corrected him.

"This is the same thing as what Max calls character?" Pavel asked, genuinely interested.

"Almost the same," Charlotte said. "Patina is something that evolves over time, Pavel. It's all the nicks and scrapes, the scars that show that a piece has lived."

"Is this why you are attracted to this furniture, Charlotte?" Pavel asked, moving across the seat. "Because of its patina?"

"Yes, that's part of it." Charlotte, replied, lost, for a minute, in her own passion. "Most people see these signs of life as damage, as something that diminishes the beauty of a piece."

"And you don't?" Pavel asked, lowering his window.

"No. These pieces have been around for centuries. The damage is part of their identity. It's why I hate pieces that are too restored."

"Can you give me an example, I mean, of too much restored?"

"Well, it's like people who inject this stuff into their wrinkles, you know, so they look younger?"

Pavel nodded. "In Moscow, they are injecting their own stem cells into their bodies at $20,000 a shot."

"Right. And this is the problem. Because when a piece is stripped down and comes back all pretty and polished, it loses the thing that defines its beauty, which is *experience.* This is what makes it so unique."

"Charlotte, forgive me. But I believe you are quite unique, too. And I wonder, sometimes, if life has damaged you at all. You seem so flawless."

"Unique, maybe," she said, running her fingers through her hair and trying to defuse the tension that had sprung up between them. "But definitely not flawless. Now, are we going to eat tomorrow night?"

"Yes, I will spend tonight in Jersey with my family. But I've made reservations at Per Se for 8 o'clock. Does this sound good?"

"This sounds marvelous, Pavel," Charlotte said, giving him a small smile. "Now please ask your driver to stop so I can get out and find something to wear."

When the limo stopped on 58th Street and Fifth, Charlotte jogged toward 6th Avenue where a new Internet café had been tucked into the ground floor of a high rise office building. *I'll just do some surfing*, she told herself, waiting in line for a terminal. She was too smart to take any stupid risks, especially now. But after sitting down and scrolling through her e-mail inbox, her heart fluttered. The woman with the silver had actually answered her.

Subj: Tiffany place settings
Date: 10/15/2009
From: gcraven@gmail.com
To: Kate.cat@hotmail.com
Dear Kate:
The silver is just taking up space and I'd like to get rid of it. But

I am a little nervous about selling to strangers. Could you tell me a bit about yourself or give me some kind of reference? My cell phone number is 917-865-9806.
Thanks,
Gina

Charlotte improvised a quick resume and e-mailed back. She wrote down the woman's number and logged off. Picking up her purse, she decided to walk two blocks to Bergdorf's on Fifth Avenue. Maybe she'd even call Gina from a payphone and set up a time to meet. Charlotte was good on the phone.

31

Charlotte's mouth was dry and her neck was itching. What she'd wanted seemed so simple: a three-ply cream silk shirt to go with the velvet shawl that she'd picked up years ago in Rajasthan. The shawl was magnificent. A six-foot piece of burgundy velvet, hand-embroidered with seed pearls and gem-like crystals. But after an hour at Bergdorf's, she was still searching. God! How she hated shopping for clothing, the sifting through racks and racks of clothing and getting undressed in rooms that were probably wired for everything, including sound.

"It's part of the process, Charlotte," Vicky had said the last time Charlotte complained. *When had shopping, like grieving, become a process, anyway?* Probably at the same time the sales help had become "associates." And who the hell was Vicky to talk about *process*? Nobody with Adult Attention Deficit Disorder had the patience for "process." For Vicky, it was all about *evading*, not enduring process. When her "associate" Samantha tapped on the dressing room door with yet another armful of suggestions, Charlotte barked, "No more!"

Twenty minutes later, Charlotte was still stuck in a cab on her way downtown. Madly scratching at her neck, she listened to her cell messages: Anna congratulating her on the sale, Darryl's handlers at the fashion company, and Rita.

Rita was furious. "Call me the minute you get this, Charlotte. That library desk you bought is a FAKE! Do you hear me... $700,000 and it's a fake!"

Charlotte's hands were shaking as she drummed her feet on the floor.

"Driver, driver," she shouted. "You should've taken Fifth. It's sequential lights. I could have been home by now!"

The driver just kept talking into the headset of his cell phone.

"Stop! Stop right now!" she said, banging on the plastic window that separated her from the front seat.

Speed-dialing Rita, she jumped out of the cab and raced across 51st Street toward the Lexington Avenue subway. Ignoring the red light, she nearly knocked a one-legged messenger off his bike. Both of them looked at one another, stunned and angry, then laughed.

"Sorry! I'm so sorry!" Charlotte said, bending down to pick up his bag. "I was in such a hurry, I didn't look."

"Yeah! I understand," the messenger said, rearranging his bag and walkie-talkie. "We're all in a hurry, ain't we?"

As the subway rattled through the darkness, Charlotte

played her favorite "what if" game. What if Rita knew that every time she invited Charlotte into her house and closed the door, she locked herself in with a murderer? What if she knew that every time she bitched about the height of a bedside table, or the color of a swatch, or the weave of a Dhurri carpet, Charlotte fantasized about smashing her head in with a poker? Just withholding this information from Rita made Charlotte feel powerful and generous. She wasn't Rita's lackey, she was a giver and a taker of life. How did Rita's billions compare to that kind of omnipotence?

32

When you worship appearances, especially your own, it doesn't pay to skimp on closet space. Which was why Rita, her closet consultant, and a team of Irish mill workers had devoted the same painstaking detail and exorbitant sum of money to the building of her refrigerated sycamore closets as the faithful once devoted to the construction of cathedrals. (Rita also rented an additional climate-controlled storage unit in upstate Connecticut "for the good stuff.") The clothing in town was arranged alphabetically and chronologically by designer, color, and season. One morning the previous spring, Charlotte had seen Rita respond to the discovery of a single Prada dress out of place with the same level of hysteria as she once did to the discovery of cysts on her ovaries and the news of 3,000 people killed downtown.

Rita was whining. "I'm just not sure, Diane. It has to be *exactly* right. This is the first time the Johnsons have invited us to the opera." The clothing stylist reassured her client with a steady stream of quiet patter. It was a familiar technique. The patter eventually eroded away at the objections and a choice was made.

"Charlotte, come in here, please," Rita begged. "I want to know what you think."

Charlotte entered the dressing room. "You look lovely, Rita!" she said, winking at the stylist.

"Really?"

"Absolutely. The blue is the same color as your eyes. And I love the ruching."

"Alright, Diane. Tell Oscar I'll take it. Just make sure the alterations are done by Wednesday."

As Diane unzipped the gown and Rita stepped out from its cocoon of foamy azure satin, she looked at Charlotte's reflection in the wall of full-length mirrors.

"Why have you got a pin in her hand, Charlotte?"

"I'm going to show you how to tell the fake from the real thing, Rita. I'll meet you in the bedroom."

Rita's eyes lit up. This was the thing about obsessive compulsives; they weren't just perfectionists; they were always *right*. "But the desk you bought is downstairs in the library," she said.

"I know," Charlotte said, turning and heading out of the dressing room. "But the fake is in your bedroom."

She was hauling the Venetian Baroque chest of drawers out from against the wall when Rita jogged into the room.

"What are you doing?" she squawked. "Caroline picked

that out for me, Charlotte. It was owned by the same Italian family for three centuries."

"Maybe," Charlotte said, pushing her straight pin into a wormhole in the diamond patterned marquetry. Rita came over and huddled over the chest as Charlotte pulled out the pin.

"Go ahead, Rita. You do it."

Rita stuck the pin in and out. "What's your point, Charlotte?"

"The point is, Rita, the only worm at work here is Caroline. That little tunnel shouldn't be straight. It should be sort of irregular. That's how nature creates those holes. And let me show you something else," Charlotte said, moving around towards the back of the chest of drawers.

Rita was following her, more curious than angry.

"Look at the wood. It's walnut, the same as the rest of the piece, right?"

"Obviously," Rita replied, smirking.

"It shouldn't be," Charlotte said. "It should be a cheaper wood."

"What are you talking about?" Rita pouted, peering at the back.

"If this were three centuries old, the guy who made it would have used a cheaper wood for the back. Something like pine. Same for the inside. That's how they did it then."

"Oh my God!" Rita said, lurching back and leaning against the wall. "What else?"

"Do you really want to know?"

"Abe'll murder me. That piece cost him more than the one you bought."

Charlotte took Rita by the hand and circled towards the front of the chest.

"See these drawers?" she asked, kneeling down and pulling one of them out. "Feel the bottom."

Rita ran her hands across the bottom.

"Smooth, right?"

Rita nodded.

"They should be rough. And again, the wood should be different than the outside. And cheaper."

Rita pulled her hand away as if she had been burned. Which, of course, she had. By Caroline.

"Now check the keyhole."

Rita's whole body sagged.

"Do you see any trace of polish, any scrapes?"

"No."

"After three centuries, don't you think there should be some sign of somebody cleaning it?"

"Oh God, Charlotte! Don't tell me any more, please!"

Sitting in a heap on the carpet, a mere shadow of her former know-it-all self, Charlotte almost felt sorry for Rita.

"How old do you think it really is?" she asked, glumly rising to her feet.

"You mean, how young?" Charlotte replied. "Some parts of it are probably very old. You wouldn't believe what these craftsmen can do in England and China."

"China?" Rita groaned.

"Yeah. There's a repro guy on my block downtown. Until a month ago when he got thrown in jail for arms and drug dealing, he was bringing in stuff that even fooled the antique experts at H.M. Luther."

Her mission accomplished, Charlotte patted Rita on the hand and passed her the straight pin. "Use it to test the piece I bought in the library, Rita."

"You promise you won't say anything to Abe, right?"

"Of course, I promise," Charlotte said, as they walked, arm in arm, towards the stairs. Secrets were like money in the bank for Charlotte. They gave her a nice bit of leverage when clients got out of control.

"Not that I really care, Rita," Charlotte said as the housekeeper helped her into her Searle parka. "But who told you my piece was a fake?"

Rita blushed. "It was the color consultant."

"Tell her to stick to paint chips in the future, will you?" Charlotte said, making no attempt to disguise her ear-to-ear grin.

33

Charlotte sang to herself as she rubbed a pearl-sized dot of La Prairie moisturizer onto her face, a barely-there layer of bronze powder to her cheeks, and a bit of Arden Eight Hour Cream on her lips.

Thank God I've always avoided the sun, she thought, searching for nonexistent pores in the mirror. What was it Vicky had raved about before leaving for the safari? Collagens derived from human foreskins? *Whose foreskins?* She'd wondered. Where do you get human foreskins? From dead men? Did husbands pluck them off the penises of defeated rivals? Did they buy them from *moyels*, the people who performed ritual circumcisions? Just the idea of it made Charlotte sick. Tying her freshly-shampooed hair up in a velvet hair-band, she was still singing when she hit the sidewalk.

Before taking off on her power walk, Charlotte hurried over to West Broadway and slid a quarter into the payphone. She had already left three messages on Gina's cell. When she heard an actual voice, she blanked for a moment.

"Gina?

Silence.

"Gina? It's Kate, from Craigslist."

"Ahhh, yes." The high-pitched voice sounded like a child. "Listen, I think I've changed my mind. I don't want to sell the silver, after all."

"I understand," Charlotte replied, softly. "You're probably as nervous as I am, right? I mean, I sold a St. Laurent last week and..."

"Oh My God!" the woman squealed. "Couture or ready-to-wear?"

Charlotte laughed. "Couture, of course. Fall 1977."

"Tell me you're joking, Kate! Wasn't that the year of his Chinese Collection?"

"Yup. One of his best, I think. Anyway, I got $12,000 for it."

"I'm swooning, I'm positively swooning. Couture is the one thing I just cannot talk Steve into buying for me. 'It's absurd, darling,' he says to me. '$50,000 for a stupid dress.'"

"Ah well," Charlotte giggled. "Men have a lot to learn, don't they?"

"They sure do," Gina sighed. "So. Would you be willing to pay cash, do you think?"

Charlotte grinned. Thank God for greed! "Oh definitely! I only take cash, myself. And if you're anxious about letting me in, I could meet you at Starbucks or something. That story in the *Post* really spooked me."

"No! No!" the girl said, back-tracking. "Don't be silly. You don't sound like a killer. I mean, how many killers wear couture St. Laurent, right?" She laughed. "But listen, Steve's away and I'm going up to my ashram for a week. Could you come to the house next Tuesday? I'm done with yoga at noon."

"Oh wow!" Charlotte exclaimed. "You're into yoga, too? I think it saved my life. I mean, I'm so hooked I carry my mat around with me everywhere."

"Me, too! Me, too!" the girl echoed, delightedly. "This might actually be fun."

Charlotte scribbled down the Tribeca address. "Is there a doorman, Gina?"

"He was fired last week. Turns out the guy was a convicted *felon*." Of course, Gina wanted her to know that it was *usually* a doorman building, not some yet-unrenovated *walk-up*.

"Jesus!" Charlotte commiserated. "What a bore for you."

"Yeah. But luckily there's a new guy starting at the end of the month."

Charlotte smiled.

34

How the hell the concierge at the Mandarin Oriental had

confused Per Se with Pure, the vegan joint on Irving Place, was a question Charlotte would address later. The restaurant served no animal products and no food heated above 115 degrees—in other words, *raw*. For now, she sat back and surveyed the room. There was Jessica Davies Morton, too taut to talk, her skin stretched tighter than a jib in a gale. Her husband, Mort, had just succeeded in running some gigantic toy company into the ground and walking away with $300 million. "Failure is a great teacher," he'd said to reporters with a wink, as he left the company's corporate headquarters.

At the sound of Pavel's voice, her focus quickly shifted back to her own table. He was bellowing at the Armani-clad waiter cowering behind her.

"Is my problem, you say? All I ask for is a piece of bread."

The restaurant was so silent, even the din of cutlery had died.

"Sorry, sir. I told you. We don't serve bread here. Our raw vegetables, nuts and seeds are—"

"HA!" Pavel shouted, wheezing with laughter. "Nuts and seeds? This is food for the fucking gulag."

Charlotte smiled. How did one explain paying eighty bucks a plate for seeds and uncooked fruits and vegetables to a guy whose mother had probably spent thirty years waiting in line to buy a loaf of stale bread? In the meantime, Pavel had lowered his voice and reached for her hand.

"Listen, I apologize, Charlotte. Really. But the first time I came to America eight years ago, I borrowed a friend's video camera. We went and shot thirty minutes of footage in the meat department at Gristedes. Because I had never seen so much meat. So you see, it is absurd to me, this idea of..."

"Pavel, it's OK," Charlotte replied, squeezing his hand, "I don't really get it, either."

"Who are these crazy peoples, anyways?" he asked, turning his head and staring at the packed room.

As the chatter in the restaurant resumed and Charlotte ordered tomato cucumber pâtés and truffle mushroom pasta made from coconut paste, she filled Pavel in with a fast and funny run-down of the local "purists."

Oh Christ. There was Deena. Charlotte ducked as Pavel gulped from his glass of organic wine.

"See that woman over there, Pavel?" she said, sliding her eyes off towards a remote corner where a group of middle-aged "girls" pecked away at their plates. "The one in the middle of the banquette?"

"Yes..." he replied, taking another healthy gulp. "What about her?"

There was something crow-like about them, Charlotte thought, forgetting for a moment that she wasn't alone. *All sleek and beaky in black.*

"Charlotte, hello, Charlotte!" Pavel was plucking at her sleeve.

"I am so, so sorry, Pavel," she said. "Where was I?"

"You were telling me about that woman on the banquette," he replied, looking at her curiously.

"Right. Well, she was a client of mine, wife of a hedge fund guy. She used to conduct meetings while doing laps in her pool. I would sit on the edge with my books of swatches and my photos, waiting, and she would be doing these breaststrokes, back and forth, gasping for air before she reached my end. Then I would flash the swatch and down she'd go, head in, head out."

Pavel waved the waiters away with his hand.

Encouraged, Charlotte plunged ahead. "Anyway, one afternoon, her husband pulls me aside outside the pool room.

"'I need you to do something for me, Charlotte,' he says. He's nervous, I can tell. There'd already been a hundred change orders on the job. 'Sure, Anthony,' I tell him. 'What is it?'

"'My wife, she farts,' he says. 'She farts all the time and the smell is unbearable.'"

Pavel grinned.

"This is a chic woman, Pavel. I mean, her face is all over the *New York Times* Styles Section every week. So I look at him and I say, 'Well, listen, Anthony. That's terrible. But I don't know what you want me to do about it.'

"'I want you to build her a bathroom that is 100% soundproof and smell-proof,' he says. 'If you don't, we're going to end up divorced.'"

"And how on earth do you do such a thing?" Pavel asked, poking, suspiciously, at his "pâté."

"We installed a spring-loaded drop seal at the bottom of the door. You close the door, a little pin gets hit by the jam, and down drops the seal. I'd like to say they lived happily ever after, but the husband had an affair with the carpenter and the wife took off with her daughter's personal trainer."

Pavel looked perplexed. "The carpenter? Was a man?" he asked.

"Yeah, ends up the husband was gay."

"Well, at least this story proves your clients are human, Charlotte."

"Almost human," she answered.

"So how do you deal with them?" Pavel asked, as he played with the little that was left of his pâté. "Most of the rich I have met here in America are not just wealthy, they are also beautiful and famous."

Putting down her knife and fork, Charlotte stared into the distance. "A long time ago," she said, "I empathized with very rich women. Having too much money, like being too beautiful, can be atrociously lonely."

Pavel snorted.

"It's true. Some of my clients … hell, lots of the women in this room, go for days touched only by people who are paid to touch them: hairdressers, personal trainers, masseurs, doctors. They never cook a meal, or wash a dish, or bathe a baby. They've forgotten there's no such thing as easy money, Pavel. And they're paying for it!"

Pavel squirmed in his chair. "Surely, there are worse problems than this, Charlotte?" he asked. "Should I pity them? These people you talk about are why we had a revolution in Russia. They are despicable, selfish. So again, I must ask you. How do you deal with them?"

Charlotte sat there, at a sudden loss for words. *I murder them*! She wanted to blurt out.

"I treat them fearlessly," she said. "I make fun of them. I show them that I'm not the slightest bit intimated. Or at least that's what I used to do when I was younger and stronger and less angry. And it worked like a charm," Charlotte said, touching the tiny Eiffel Tower on her Craigslist bracelet and digging into her coconut paste pasta. "They were completely seduced."

"Is this what you do with me?" Pavel asked, tasting his dish, and sitting back in his chair eyeing her.

"I don't know enough about you to make fun of you," she replied.

"What would you like to know?" he asked.

Do you kill people? flashed through her mind. "You scare me," she said.

"I scare many people, Charlotte. It is a trick I use to survive. But you have no reason to feel that way."

"Feeling has nothing to do with reason, Pavel. Surely, you realize that?"

"So what else do you feel about me?" he asked, taking a last delicate bite of his mushroom squash. She didn't know a big man could be so delicate.

"Listen, this is a relationship about work," she replied. "And I'm very rigid when it comes to my boundaries." She could feel the flush of heat rising up her neck, thinking of her original plan to seduce and use him. "But I would like to know why your family is safer in Jersey."

"Ahh, Yes!" said Pavel, pushing his plate away. "It must seem strange. But I am one of six men I know who boards the same Delta flight from Moscow every month. The answer to your question is simple: family makes me an easy target. And I cannot afford to put them at risk. What is it, you say? Better safe than sorry?"

"Yes! So how come they can't live at the dacha? In the country?"

"I bought my house from the family of a man who was

killed on a Moscow street corner. I was smart enough not to ask why. We Russians can be as pitiless to one another as we are to the earth we once cherished."

As if to distract her, he reached down into his pocket and pulled out a color photograph. "This is the latest picture of the dacha," he said, sliding it across the table.

Charlotte picked it up and exhaled. "Whew!" she said. "I bet astronauts can see your wall from space…"

"Russians love walls, Charlotte. When I move into my village, I gave the priest some money for his church. The church was a mess. The peasants had been using it to store feed for their cows and horses. It stank. But the very the first thing the priest built was a wall…"

"If there's one thing I know all about, Pavel. It's walls."

"Yes, Charlotte. I realize that. Now, let me get the bill and you can tell me all about them."

As Pavel eyed the head waiter, Charlotte wrapped herself up in her velvet shawl. She thought, *I can't believe I'm talking*. Like John, the homeless man, if she wasn't talking to clients, Charlotte spent most of her time talking to herself. But tonight, she felt as if Pavel had cast a spell again; as if she were, somehow, enchanted. Pulling the shawl around her like a shroud, she shivered. Talking was dangerous.

35

Charlotte had been taught to submit gracefully. But the resentment that lay just beneath the surface made each and every act of submission, no matter how trivial, feel like rape.

So when they'd arrived back at the loft, Pavel had sensed her reluctance. Unlike other men, he hadn't rushed her. He'd sat, sipping a cognac, patiently waiting for her to come to him.

"Would you tell me another fairytale, Pavel?" she asked, moving closer to him on the couch and stretching out her legs. "About your dacha."

"Ahh! My beloved dacha!" he replied. "I hope you are not another one of those Americans who always think of that ridiculous Egyptian in Dr. Zhivago? What was his name?"

"Sharif. Omar Sharif," Charlotte said.

"Right. I will tell you about my banya that I built with my own hands," he said, briefly touching her hair. "But first you must relax. Close your eyes, Charlotte."

She obeyed.

"In the big house, I did nothing but pay people to spend my money. It has a swimming pool and fancy Finnish sauna. This is for business. But the banya, this small wooden cabin, is only for me and my closest friends."

Pavel's voice was so deep, so mellifluous, she felt as if she were being carried away. As his hands slowly massaged her neck, she purred.

"Good! You are getting relaxed, Charlotte. The banya is made of cedarwood. Inside, I have made a simple room for drinking vodka and hot tea with jam. There are pegs nailed into the wall for hanging my robes and towels. They are all white and soft. From Sweden. You cannot imagine what luxury these towels are for me, Charlotte. You are asleep?" he asked, gently pinching her arm.

"No, just dreaming, Pavel. Tell me more," Charlotte said.

"When I sit in my sauna, I like it very, very hot. So I dip

a big wooden spoon into a bucket filled with water from my river."

Charlotte smiled. "*Your* river, Pavel?"

"That is correct. Before it was the people's river. But now it is on my property. So it is *my* river," Pavel replied. "I throw this water on hot rocks. You can hear the hiss, the sizzle of heat. I slap my back with a broom of birch twigs. It stings. The soap and the slap of leaves. But it feels good. Then I climb wooden steps and soak in a deep wooden tub with cool river water."

Pavel's hands had now slipped discreetly beneath her shirt. He was gently kneading the muscles in the small of her back. How did he know exactly where she ached? Charlotte sighed.

"Are you still here, Charlotte?" he asked.

"I'm melting."

"After the banya, I go out and plunge into my river. I put my head under this ice-cold still clean rushing river. I hold onto a rusty old ring on the dock because the river flow is so strong. The river is also full of weeds. Weeds that can strangle people who are drunk."

Pavel gently squeezed the flesh above her buttocks. She was so relaxed, he could have strangled her right then and she wouldn't have even bothered to struggle.

"I come up from the river, naked. I am dripping wet and reborn. Clean and pure like a baby after baptism. This is how we Russian men get clean after another day of hurting or cheating other people. People who are sometimes friends. We must do this or we drown ourselves."

Languid with the heat from the fireplace and the strength

of his stroking hands, Charlotte touched his face.

"I will tell you one more thing about the banya. And then we will move onto other things. It is in the banya where a Russian man is *almost* vulnerable. We do not even have a word for vulnerable in our language, Charlotte. But with the steam and the heat and the sweat, secrets are revealed, souls are swindled, lies are uncovered."

Pavel sighed. "There are millions who have returned to the church in Russia. They have bumps on their foreheads from kissing the cold stone and praying. But me? I will always return to my banya."

During his story, Pavel's hands had navigated their way, slowly, so slowly, through her layers of clothing, moving in a series of slow-motion fits and starts.

"Please, hurry," Charlotte finally said, arms over her head and legs sprawled open on the couch. "I want you to hurry."

"There is no hurry," he said, fingers fluttering like a moth's wings over the hollow space between her shoulder blades. "Just breathe, Charlotte. Breathe."

She closed her eyes and obeyed.

With other men, Charlotte had also always insisted on keeping some piece of clothing on, even if it was only a lacy French bra. It comforted her, somehow. It made her feel less exposed. But Pavel had understood her need for darkness and her fear of being naked. By the time they had gone into her bedroom and he had brought her to a second climax, it was she who had snapped the light on.

"I want to see you," she'd said. "I want to see where you like to be touched." And he'd shown her.

Before Pavel had drifted off to sleep, Charlotte ran her

hands over her own body, amazed at the smoothness of the curves, at the sensitivity of areas like the nape of her neck and the inside of her calves.

As he began to snore, her eyes traveled over his taut muscles; his knotted arms and long, delicate fingers. Even his toenails were buffed. When he abruptly shifted position, stretching out his arms, she wriggled away. It was then that she saw the tattoo. It was the silhouette of a sailing ship, hidden in the crook of his left arm. Her heart leapt as he turned over and she closed her eyes, pretending to be asleep.

She woke up at three in the morning, her pulse racing. It was the usual nightmare with her mother chasing her. Snapping the switch off on her bedside lamp, she sat up in the dark and saw herself as a small child, shrieking and clutching something tightly in her fists; something that was all over the sheets and pillowcases of her bed. But what was it? Not blood. Charlotte was sure of that.

Pavel's kiss startled her so badly she nearly screamed.

"What is it, Charlotte. What's happened?"

"Nothing. It's nothing."

"Please, Charlotte. Allow me to comfort you."

She stiffened and pulled away.

"Or if not comfort you then listen, Charlotte. I am a very good listener."

And to her surprise, she told him the truth. "It was a dream about this thing that happened to me when I was a kid," Charlotte replied, pulling the sheet around her body, hugging herself. Charlotte was so stupefied at the intensity of the memory that her teeth were chattering.

With his eyes shut, Pavel's fingers traced the outline of his tattoo, following the shape of its billowing sails, caressing the waves that lapped up against the ship's prow. *As if by touching it,* Charlotte thought, *he might find himself transported elsewhere.* Even his voice sounded as if it were coming from far away.

"Do you know what is the hardest thing for humans to forgive, Charlotte?" he asked.

"Hurting children," she instantly replied, seeing that image of herself in bed as a child.

"Perhaps. But I think it is forgiveness itself."

Charlotte just shook her head.

"You think it doesn't make sense? But if you forgive even the closest friend one too many times, the friend will become an enemy. It has happened to me. Because to accept forgiveness, you must first accept that you are loved. Do you see?"

"Not really," Charlotte answered, pulling the sheet so tightly around her body, she could hardly move.

"Ambulance drivers in Italy used to wear black hoods. So that the people they saved would not feel they owed them a debt of gratitude. It works the same way for people who are forgiven. There is a debt that grows and grows. Only if you are very lucky does the other person not feel resentment. It may be guilt. It may be the burden of debt. But in the end, it all becomes too much to bear."

When Pavel closed his arm, the tattoo of the ship disappeared, almost as if it had caught a gust of wind and sailed away. "Enough of my mysterious philosophy, Charlotte," he said. "Why have you not asked about my tattoo?"

"I didn't want to pry," she answered.

"The ship is a symbol of my love of freedom," Pavel said, quietly. "And my regret at its loss. Simple, no?" he added with a smile.

"Not so simple at all, Pavel." Charlotte replied, afraid to look into his eyes. "But I don't want to think about any of this right now. Help me forget." And Pavel did.

36

Like the steel rivets on a ship's waterproof door that pop, one by one, as the pressure builds, Charlotte felt her head begin to pound as her stomach muscles cramped. It was six on Wednesday morning and she was in her bath. The small television in the armoire where she kept her towels was on with the sound muted. Lulled by the heat, she'd caught only the tail end of the banner running across the bottom of the screen. *Witness to the murder of Amy Webb...*

As she grabbed a towel and climbed out of the tub, she nearly lost her balance. Reaching for the remote control, she turned up the volume and paced, as restless as a cat, waiting for the commercials to end. The anchorwoman on Channel 1 fiddled with her earpiece and gazed into the camera.

"Last night, police report they received a call at 1-800-577-TIPS from a woman who claims to have seen someone leaving the East Side residence of Amy Webb on the Friday afternoon she was murdered. Apparently, the woman, a housekeeper from Croatia, did not come forward until now as she was frightened of being deported. She spoke to authorities through an interpreter. We'll have more news on this story as it develops."

Willing herself to remain calm, Charlotte retraced her movements on that afternoon. It had been pouring rain. She distinctly remembered that. And it was nearly dark. Her head was hidden in the hood of her parka. What could the woman have possibly seen that would endanger her? Hearing a hesitant knock on the bathroom door, Charlotte picked up her bottle of Caleche, paused, and placed a few dabs on her pulse points. Looking hard in the mirror, she practiced her most radiant smile, and put on a bathrobe. At times like this, façade was all she had to hold onto. "I'm coming, Pavel," she shouted. "I'm coming."

As he leaned down to give her a kiss on the mouth, she felt just the tiniest prickle of regret. She'd opened herself up to this man and—related or not—now her life was unraveling. Her carefully constructed world was falling apart. And Pavel already seemed to have one foot out the door. Chatting away in Russian on his cell phone while picking up his coat, he did little more than exchange pleasantries before promising to call and set up a week for her visit to Moscow.

After his cursory kiss good-bye, Charlotte sat slumped in a chair at her kitchen table, sipping her coffee. She thought of Max and his depth charge metaphor; of how she'd lived for so many years without ever thinking of her childhood, as if it had simply ceased to exist once it was over. Suddenly, she was besieged by memories that were almost cinematic in their detail.

She remembered her twelfth birthday party. For once, her mother had seemed almost eager to share in the planning. She had suggested a costume theme. After the class trip to the Egyptian wing at the Metropolitan Museum of Art, Charlotte came up with the idea of ancient Egypt. She would go as Cleopatra. The day of the party, Charlotte went off to school, ecstatic and anxious.

When Charlotte got home, she'd walked through the door with her eyes closed. She'd imagined the hall transformed into a pharaoh's tomb with golden caskets and hieroglyphics on the walls. But there was nothing. The hallway was empty. "Mom! Mom!" she had yelled out, racing from room to room.

"Where are you?"

Her mother appeared from her bedroom with an open book in her hand. "Slow down, Charlotte," she'd said, annoyed. "Whatever is the matter?"

"It's my birthday, Mom. All my friends are coming over for my party. And I don't see any decorations."

Her mother had just made a clucking sound with her tongue. "Surely not, Charlotte. The caterers are coming next Wednesday, not today."

Forty girls had rung the bell that afternoon while Charlotte hid in her room. No one at school spoke to her for a week. They tittered when they raced past her in the hallways. This was when Charlotte had her first stomachache. She lay in the nurse's room for hours, holding her belly, moaning.

Thinking about it now, she tried to imagine Vicky pulling a similarly cruel trick on her daughter. Vicky who had shelled out half a million dollars for a "Jewels and Jeans" birthday party for her thirteen-year-old. All thirty girls got goody bags with fourteen-karat gold name necklaces from Jacob the Jeweler and a full day of spa treatments at Rapture.

Vicky's daughter had worn a pair of Swarovski crystal-studded Diesels and a $400,000 ruby and diamond tiara from Fred Leighton. Although the tiara had been borrowed, there was something about the party that seemed scarier to Charlotte than the prom scene in the movie *Carrie*.

"What if she doesn't have a good time?" Vicky had wailed when they got together for lunch at Nello's. "What if her friends are bored?"

"Vicky, you've hired the rap singer Nas for Christ's sake. You're giving them $500 necklaces, a dinner catered by Art of Eating, and a day at a spa. What are you worried about?"

"I just want her to *love* me, that's all," she'd replied, fumbling with her napkin.

Right, Charlotte had thought, *of course*. There was nothing wrong with wanting to be loved. But why did parents assume they had to seduce their children, to woo them like lovers? It was like Darryl, the fashion designer, with her plans to create a dojo for her nine-year-old ninja. Charlotte also remembered a recent call from Deena, the client she had seen at Pure who farted and ran away with her daughter's personal trainer. For some reason, Deena assumed that Charlotte actually missed hearing her old client's voice.

"Charlotte. I need your advice so badly! You've got to help me," she'd pleaded.

"Certainly, Deena, anything." Charlotte had replied,

trying to imagine where in hell she'd find time to solve some new decorating disaster.

"It's my nineteen-year-old girl, Kyle. You remember her, right? The light of my life?"

"Sure," Charlotte said, dimly remembering the surly, overweight fourteen-year-old who'd snubbed her for months, treating her as if she were invisible.

"She's a sophomore at Wellesley. We're so proud of her. It's one of the finest all-girls colleges in the country, Charlotte."

"So what's the problem, Deena?" Charlotte asked, fixated on a guy texting on a cell phone while his tongue moved in and around a girl's mouth. *Great multitasking*, Charlotte thought to herself.

"Sorry, what did you say?" she asked.

"I said, my daughter wants a gender reassignment, Charlotte. She says if we won't pay for it, she'll go to Thailand."

"A what? Charlotte squeaked. "Forgive me, Deena. But I have no idea what you're talking about.

"A sex change," Deena whispered. "It's called gender reassignment now."

"Holy shit!" The expletive flew out of Charlotte's mouth before she realized it. "Did you tell her that this *reassignment* isn't exactly like switching from science to French or turning in a hatchback for a sedan at Avis? It's permanent, for god's sake."

"I'm beside myself, that's all I can say. I figured the college would put an end to it. It's *all girls*, Charlotte. If she turns into a boy, she'd have to transfer."

"That seems like the least of your problems, Deena. Have you tried saying *no*?"

"Yes. And I got nowhere. And now the damn college is

changing their rules. In *her* favor, Charlotte. They're saying if you come in as a girl and change your mind, or grow a penis or whatever, they'll graduate you as a boy."

"Deena, I don't know what to say. Except to tell her the answer is 'no' again. Tell her you're perfectly willing to pay the $53,000 tuition. But you have to draw the line somewhere..."

This was the dilemma, wasn't it? thought Charlotte.

Parents didn't know how to say "no" anymore. They didn't dare. Only children did.

Charlotte believed that children often longed to hear the word. There was safety and certainty in the word "no." It implied that there were rules; that there was someone to rely on who was wiser, older, smarter. And what about sending tweenies off on private jets for shop-til-you-drop tours of Paris, then shipping them off to a $70,000 "tough love" wilderness camp in Utah? Vicky had "shared" her latest plans for her daughter before leaving for Botswana. How tough could love be at seventy grand?

Was it all the fat from their asses being injected into their faces that had turned parenting upside down—that had made rich, educated grown-ups so intimidated by their children that Charlotte had seen mothers down on their knees on the street, *begging* and *bribing* kids to stop screaming? Is this what had turned so many toddlers and teenagers into tyrants? Is this why daughters dreamt of being as thin as famine victims or becoming boys, while sons annihilated themselves with drugs and booze?

Making a desultory effort to clean up her kitchen after her solitary breakfast, Charlotte thought, once again, of her own mother; of how many ugly betrayals and humiliations there had been. Wandering off towards her bedroom, she stepped into her closet and reached for a wide, pinstripe Comme des Garcons cotton shirt, a pair of orange silk Turkish pants, and a Beene scarf.

Charlotte knew that she had to stop the thinking, the *thawing*. She had to work. Pavel had opened up an account in her name at Commerce Bank to cover the decorating expenses. "I trust you," he'd said, holding her hands in his before giving her the checkbook. The opening balance was small, only $200,000. The rest would be wired from an account in Cyprus. Charlotte had been tempted to "borrow" $8,000 to pay off her Amex debts from this account. She'd cover it with mark-ups. But she resisted.

Pavel had paid Max for the cassa panca himself. But Charlotte had covered thousands of dollars more from her own account: fabrics at the D&D, the Murano lamp, and the restored commode that she'd bought from the new dealer downtown. Then there was the $40,000 for curtain hardware: the custom-made poles, finials, brackets, and rings. She'd spend a couple of hours tallying up her totals and then, maybe, head out to East Hampton.

A new client had offered her a limo and two nights at the Maidstone Inn. It would be good to get of town. There'd been a message on her machine from Gina, too.

"I can't wait to see you, Charlotte," she'd said. "So please don't forget our appointment. Oh. And bring cash!"

37

The new client's chauffeur was driving her back from East Hampton when she saw the sign. Stuck at a dead halt somewhere between exits 31 and 35, she erupted into a burst of laughter. There it was on the side of the road: "Adopt-A-Highway. Litter Control Next One Mile. Rita and Abe Brickman." Rita had mentioned hiring a publicist; but this was just too good.

Sticking her name on the L.I.E. where every social-climbing slob in an S.U.V would see it on their way back from the beach! And you'd think they could afford to clean up *two* miles, wouldn't you? One mile made them seem so cheap. Dabbing at her eyes, Charlotte phoned her branch of the Commerce Bank to check her balance. There was still no money in her account. Pavel had handled the wire transfer before he left for Moscow. She'd stood right next to him when he made the call. So what had happened? He couldn't have lied, could he?

Commerce was the only bank in town open seven days a week. Dumping her bag in the hallway of the loft, she rushed back downstairs, and hailed a cab. A conversation with the bank manager uptown accomplished nothing.

"I've checked the account twice, madam."

Jesus. She hated that word, *madam*.

"If he sent it when he said he did, it would be here by now."

"I'd like to speak with your manager, please." Charlotte

had said, twisting around in her chair to look for someone more important; someone who hadn't bought a suit straight off the rack at Kmart.

"I am the manager, madam," he'd retorted, pointing to the plaque on his desk. "See? Vice president?"

"I can read, thank you," Charlotte had replied, haughtily.

"All I can suggest is that you contact the party involved and ask him when the transfer was sent. Maybe he had the wrong routing number or something."

Ignoring him, she pulled on her coat and marched off towards the door.

Shit! she thought. Charlotte tried Pavel's cell for the third time. *Where is he?*

Even the walk back downtown depressed her. The tall buildings that loomed above her cast cold, dark shadows. Her rhythm was off and she'd fallen out of sync with the traffic lights. This city that she so often turned to for solace and comfort, suddenly felt suffocatingly close and small. What was the matter with her? When she got home, she saw a guy in camouflage pants, peering into the side mirror of a car. He was squeezing his pimples. How could a guy do something as intimate and ugly as squeeze pimples in public? It revolted her.

"Hey! Charlotte, Charlotte!" John the homeless guy was shuffling up the block, dropping his papers, holding his hands out to stop her.

"Christ!" she muttered. *He stinks.* Charlotte's bad mood took over; she didn't care if he was homeless. She just wished to hell he'd take a shower.

"What is it, John?" she snarled. "I don't have much time."

Recoiling as if slapped, he lowered his eyes. "Sorry, sorry,

Charlotte. Just want you know the UPS man was looking for you yesterday. He left a package at the dry cleaner."

Charlotte felt so guilty, she palmed him a twenty.

"Thanks, John. And it's me who's sorry. Bad day, you know?"

"No problem, Charlotte. I have bad days, too," John said, as he shuffled back down the block.

Jogging over to the cleaners, she sighed with relief. She liked Brian, the UPS guy who delivered to her door. He was New York Irish, like the old cops and firemen. He also had some kind of oral fixation. In ten years, she'd never seen him without a piece of gum in his mouth. He liked sucking lollipops, too. The problem was, he talked too much. And today, she was in no mood for talk.

After a few quick words with Kim (whose knowledge of English was blessedly limited to words like shirt, pant, and blouse), Charlotte lugged the box home. It was unwieldy: big but light. Recognizing the return address, its contents became even more mysterious. What could her mother possibly have sent her?

Crouching down in her hallway and puncturing the seam of the box with her pocket knife, she pulled out the note. "Dear Charlotte: Just thought you might want to have this. Mom." The handwriting was spidery. It looked like the pen was running out of ink. She began tearing out the stuffing of white tissue paper.

It must be fragile, she thought to herself. Maybe it's that

Steuben vase I asked for. When she saw what lay nestled beneath the remaining layers of tissue, she sat back and whimpered.

Putting her head between her knees, she tried to breathe in, slowly. *It couldn't be! It couldn't be!* she repeated, over and over again, as if in repeating this plea, it might suddenly disappear. But no. The hair, her own hair, was still there. Clumps of tangled, red hair, leeched of color, and brittle with age. Dragging herself along the floor towards the hall bathroom, Charlotte vomited. She vomited until there was nothing left in her stomach but clear liquid and her own bile.

If only she could sleep. And if only Anna were home. As she lay there on her bed, twisting and twitching, her eyes pinned open, she felt like a runner waiting to sprint at the sound of a starter's pistol. There was so much adrenaline pumping through her system, not even two milligrams of Ativan slowed her down. All she could see was the murderous look on her mother's face and the silvery teeth of the pinking shears, the same shears her nanny had used to cut patterns and fabric for Charlotte's doll clothes. Her hair, her beautiful hair that she brushed every night in the bathroom mirror, was falling all around her while she plugged her ears to block out the sound of snipping.

When Charlotte finally awoke, her abdomen hurt so much, she could hardly move. It was dawn. Shifting her body around beneath the sheets, she felt helpless and dirty. So dirty. The taste of vomit in her mouth nearly made her retch. She could feel the acid rise in her throat. There was still a pool of vomit in the hallway, too. She'd been too tired to even think of cleaning it up.

Closing her eyes, Charlotte imagined herself singing. She clung to the notes of this silent song as if they were a lifeline. An hour later, she picked up the phone and called Dr. Greene.

38

Like a blind person, Charlotte raised her hands to her own face and touched her features: her eyes, her nose, her cheeks. Her whole body jittered in her chair. Even her skin was clammy. Squeezing her knees tightly shut, she tried to stop the convulsive shaking. She started counting. One, two, three, four...

Dr. Greene sat across from his patient, waiting. When she realized that the pains in her stomach had subsided, she stopped shaking.

"Thank you for making time for me on a Sunday," she mumbled.

"It sounded like an emergency, Charlotte. I imagine it wasn't easy to call..."

"No," Charlotte replied, crumpling her Kleenex. "It wasn't. And I don't know what to say right now."

"You don't need to say anything if you don't want to. Sometimes, people just need to feel someone near them in times of crisis."

"Ummmm," she said, her hands gently kneading her

stomach. She was scared stiff. Literally. Afraid that the twist in her gut would return and with it, the unbearable pain.

Dr. Greene remained still, waiting for his patient's cue.

"Charlotte…"

"What's the matter with me?" she cried out. "I haven't thought of my sister in years. I didn't even remember what she looked like till yesterday."

Closing her eyes, Charlotte found herself, once again, peering over the edge of the white, wooden crib.

"She was screaming, Doctor. It just went on and on. Mother was out at a party. I don't know where nanny was. I wanted to help, you know? I wanted to tell my mother that it was me who had quieted her down and put her back to sleep."

Shifting imperceptibly in his chair, the doctor gently guided her. "What did it feel like to be with your sister? Do you remember?"

"I was never allowed to have pets at home," Charlotte replied. "So I remember how weird it felt, having something so tiny, wriggling around in my arms. And her head. Her head was so small, my hand fit right over it."

"Were you nervous?" Dr. Greene asked.

Charlotte's teeth began to chatter. "I'm so cold, Doctor."

"It's normal, Charlotte. You're not just talking here, you're feeling something."

Her eyes began to wander wildly around the room and she rocked back and forth in her chair.

"I, I…" she faltered. "I thought the bear would comfort her, you see? The way he always comforted me. So I lay her down on her stomach and went into my room to get him.

She must have quieted down. Because I left the bear in the crib and went to sleep. I wouldn't have gone to sleep if she were still crying."

"Charlotte, please forgive me. I don't want to push you if you're not ready..."

"No, I can talk, Doctor. I..."

"So what happened in the morning?"

Charlotte's lips quivered.

"I was frightened," she answered. "I mean, my father was in my sister's room. Which was unusual. And he was talking very softly. So I couldn't hear what he was saying. But he was pulling my mother away from the crib."

Charlotte's voice suddenly grew deep, harsh. She moved to the edge of her chair.

"Nanny was over at the window. When my father left the room, probably to call an ambulance or something, I started to cry."

Charlotte's knee began to bounce up and down as her eyes darted around the office. "My mother... My mother saw me. 'What happened, Mommy?' I asked her. 'What happened?'"

Charlotte slid down in her chair and hugged herself. "That's when she came at me. And she scratched my face. It stung. My fingers had blood on them when I touched my cheek. 'Get out!' she yelled. 'Get out!'

"So I ran back to my bedroom and wrapped myself up in the sheets. I could hear the sirens and the sound of all these footsteps on the stairs."

Charlotte paused and took a sip from the glass of water.

"When my mother finally came in ... it must have been

an hour later. She tiptoed over to my bed. I was so scared, I wet my pants. I just wanted to shrink into the sheets and disappear."

"'Well, Charlotte,' she said, her voice was so low I could hardly hear it. 'Your sister is dead. I think you snuck into her room and you suffocated her. But you forgot to take your bear.'"

"'I did not, Mother,' I told her. 'I did not! I'm the one who put her back to sleep.'"

Charlotte felt as if her ears had filled with water. There was a rushing sound. Her heart was beating so fast, she put her hand to her chest.

"She picked up a pair of pinking shears and she started to chop at my hair. And while she chopped, she talked. She told me that she wouldn't tell on me, that the police would never know. 'It would ruin your father's career,' she said. And then she said that she'd never wanted me, not even when I was a baby."

Charlotte stopped speaking. Her body was trembling.

In a voice so soft Dr. Greene had to lean in to hear her, she said: "She told me that every time she felt me kick her in the belly, it reminded her of what she'd lost; of all the things she'd had to give up. She said I made her feel ugly, useless."

Charlotte rubbed her eyes with her knuckles. "I couldn't move, Doctor. I just sat there in bed and waited for her to finish." Charlotte touched the top of her scalp, as if to heal the nicks, the broken skin that had been left by the tips of the shears thirty years before. "Then she stuck a mirror in front of my face. 'Look at yourself, Charlotte,' she said. 'Ugly and useless. That's all you'll ever be.'"

Afterwards, she remembered Nanny coming in to console her. "Your hair will grow back," she'd promised, washing away the mess of snot and tears from Charlotte's face. And her nanny was right. It did grow back. But there had been times in the years since that morning when Charlotte, shorn of everything including hair and childhood illusions, would look into a mirror and swear that there was nothing there, no reflection.

"Charlotte? Charlotte?" The voice seemed as it were coming from the bottom of the sea.

She was gripping the edge of her chair so tightly, her knuckles had turned white.

When the doctor reached out to touch her, Charlotte shrank back into her chair.

"Charlotte, I am so sorry. But we have to stop now."

Which is when Charlotte grinned. "We have to stop now!" she mimicked. "Is that all you can say after my breakthrough?"

"It's a lot to process, dear. For both of us," he replied, quietly.

She stiffened and glared at him. "Are you afraid to look at me, Doctor?"

Rummaging around his desk, the frail, elderly man picked up a prescription pad. "Of course not, Charlotte," he said, scribbling on the pad. "But I'd like to give you something to help calm you down. Just until our next session."

Snapping the brass fastener on her bag open and shut, open and shut, Charlotte stared vacantly out the office window. "Yeah, right," she, finally, said, buttoning up her cardigan and snatching the slip of paper. "Thanks for your time."

The doctor just nodded and continued writing on his legal pad.

39

Like a child who sits parked in front of television for hours and then sees the screen go dark, Charlotte felt hostile, disoriented, sluggish. Using her hand to shield her eyes from the bright sunlight, she tried to get her bearings. Even the tree-lined street outside Greene's office, a street so familiar to her she could have run its length blindfolded, felt foreign to her. She was thinking of the cartoon she'd drawn, the one her mother gave when she came to visit. There were teeth inside the mouth of the C. *Like the teeth of the shears, like C for Charlotte,* she thought. *It's me,* she thought, feeling a pang of what might have been genuine sadness. But the howl in the cartoon had been silent. And no one had ever heard her.

Pulling a silver compact out from the depths of her purse, Charlotte hesitated. She never powdered her nose or even applied lipstick in public. Such overt displays of vanity repelled her. Turning her back to the street, she stole a furtive glance in the compact and gasped. The furrows on her forehead, the deeply etched lines between her mouth and nose. She looked a hundred years old.

Wiping her face with the back of her hand, as if to erase the last hour with Dr. Greene, she vowed: *I am not going to lose control now. I will not indulge in weak, embarrassing fits of self-pity.*

When Charlotte's phone began to vibrate, she was so aware of her every movement, pulling it out from her pocket, flipping it open, and placing it next to her ear, that it felt like those slow-motion split seconds before a car crash.

"Charlotte?"

She held the phone away from her ear. Her hand was shaking.

"Charlotte! Can you hear me?" The voice at the other end was braying. Shrill.

"Yes, Mother. I'm here," Charlotte replied, robotically.

"No, Charlotte. You're there. And I need you here. I don't feel well."

"I don't feel well, either, Mother."

"I'm dizzy, light-headed."

Charlotte's chest tightened. Folding the phone neatly shut, she severed the connection. When it began to vibrate, again, she gently placed it at the bottom of her bag. The slow, deliberate movements calmed her down. Charlotte thought of the nightmares she'd had of running away from her mother and of her cartoon figure, its mouth open in a silent scream. She would take care of her mother. But right now, she needed to channel her fury somewhere more constructive.

Charlotte pulled the curtains snugly shut and collapsed on her bed. Touching the glass inside the silver picture frame, she imagined that her Aunt Dottie was there with her. *Her silence was a signal*, she thought. Proof that Dottie was listening. As she tried to explain to her aunt, this is why she had fallen so hard for Pavel. Because he was a man who could listen, too. And unlike Dr. Greene, she didn't have to pay him for it. Just the thought of Dr. Greene was unpleasant, the way he'd poked and prodded; the way he'd cut her off today.

Lying there in the dark, Charlotte caressed the soft pilled sleeves of Vicky's old sweater. Inserting her finger into a hole near the armpit, she began to tug. The yarn gave way and the hole became bigger. The sound of ripping comforted her. Gazing at the photo of her Aunt Dottie, she tried to imagine the day at Orchard Beach. She'd never been to an amusement park, not even Coney Island, but she wondered if her mother and aunt had shared a seat on the Ferris wheel; if they'd eaten pink cotton candy. She wondered who had taken the picture and thought that, perhaps, it might have been her grandfather. Charlotte's only consolation that night was her newfound realization that she was no longer afraid of her dreams. She was done with running away from her mother. There would be no more sleep-curdling visions of rooftops, silent screams, and kitchen knives.

The phone rang during breakfast. Charlotte had been sitting there, hypnotized by the silvery reflections of light on the river. Like a mirror, she'd thought, thinking of her mother. After years of being tongue-tied, she wanted answers to her questions. When she picked up the phone, the voice on the other end was breaking up.

It was Pavel.

Charlotte's muscles relaxed. She grinned.

"Charlotte, can you hear me?"

"Yes, Pavel. The connection's not great. But I hear you."

"Listen, I..."

Charlotte interrupted. "I've been trying to get you."

"I know. But there are some problems in Moscow, Charlotte. I've had to leave."

Her grin sagged. "What kind of problems?"

"I can't really talk over the phone. But my credit is frozen..." Like the vapor trails of airplanes, little tendrils of pain shot through her chest and disappeared. A vein throbbed in her temple. *Fuck!* Charlotte thought. *My money.*

"What does that mean, Pavel? Did you send the wire?"

"Look, I am trying to work it out..." He was shouting through a storm of static. She heard something about tax police and held her breath. "I'm going to be out of touch for a while. The family's meeting me and..."

"I can't hear you very well," Charlotte said, moving closer to the window in the hopes of retrieving a signal.

She heard the word "sorry" and then he was gone.

Jesus Christ. Even with her credit line, she was looking at hundreds of thousands of dollars of debt. Eighty yards of the Scalamandre silk had come in at $50,000, and that was *with* the discount. The woman making the balloon shades was charging another $15,000. She'd already started the sewing. And what about the $400,000 order for lighting? Everything was veering out of control. Anna had warned her about the Russians. She was disgusted at her own weakness, at the thought that this man had seen her naked. She had to get out of the house. Walk. At least there was Gina. Suddenly Charlotte was so excited at the prospect of seeing Gina she could feel tiny goose bumps on her arms.

The phone trilled as Charlotte dried herself off in the bathroom. Her stomach flip-flopped. Maybe it was Pavel calling back. Dropping the towel, she rushed into her bedroom and picked up.

"Charlotte?"

Just the sound of Vicky's voice annoyed her.

"Welcome back, Vicky. How was the trip?"

"Incredible, absolutely incredible. You have to come over right now and I'll tell you all about it."

"Ummmm. I'm not sure I have time," Charlotte replied. Listening to the details of other people's trips was almost as boring as listening to them talk about their dreams or their sex lives.

"Then make time, Charlotte. But forget about the trip. Wait till you hear about *last night*. It was the most moving experience of my whole life, I swear."

"Really?" Charlotte said, tuning out. "Your night with the Buddhists, right?"

"You cannot imagine. I left the house at 7:00 with no keys, no money, no phone. And everybody met me at the 72nd Street IRT."

"It hasn't been called the IRT in thirty years, Vicky!"

"Whatever. The subway, okay? Anyway, we went down to some shelters on Avenue D and rode the trains all night just like the homeless. I even talked to some of them."

"It sounds like some kind of new adventure vacation, Vicky."

"You're such a cynic, Charlotte, you know? That's your problem. This is a Buddhist tradition. They do it every year."

"Well, bravo for them, Vicky!"

But Vicky was still talking. "It was so cold out, I almost gave away my shahtoosh."

Charlotte choked. "Surely you jest, Vicky. Please don't tell me you were wearing $2,000 worth of dead Tibetan antelope hair on Avenue D? And you call yourself an f'ing Buddhist."

There was dead silence at the other end of the phone. Vicky had hung up.

Walking into the kitchen she removed a piece of soft chamois cloth from a plastic bucket under the kitchen sink. Today's moment with Gina would be perfect, she thought, stroking and polishing the poker until it gleamed. It had to be.

Feeling jubilantly alert, invincible even, she decided that she'd skip seeing Vicky—just not show up—and walk to Gina's. The walk would clear her head and help her focus. Charlotte had left the bottle of Ativan untouched on her bedside table all night. She didn't want anything to come between her and the fullness of her experience with Gina. If only others understood; if only they could see the world as she saw it, there would be no judgments. The world would applaud her courage, her *strength*.

40

Charlotte blinked. Was she hallucinating? It looked like Gina was clutching a large, claw-toothed hammer in her left hand. Her face was red and sweaty, too. Charlotte could hear the sounds of wailing from somewhere in the back of the loft. "What the hell?" she muttered, reluctant to step any farther in than the front hallway. "Make yourself comfortable, Kate," said the flustered, young blonde. "I just have to finish up some private business."

Is she kidding? Charlotte thought to herself. Had the woman hit somebody with the hammer? Her husband, maybe? Slipping out of her coat, she sat down to catch her breath. After avoiding the CCTV camera in the lobby, she'd walked up ten flights of stairs. She began to remove her fur hat, but one look in the hallway mirror changed her mind. Her hair was a wreck. She hadn't washed it in two days.

The clamor of raised voices soon had her moving on the balls of her feet towards the back.

"Please, Mrs. Craven, I swear I didn't know..."

Craning her neck, Charlotte watched as Gina pulled a young guy toward a bathroom. There were shards of porcelain all over the marble floor.

"You didn't know not to use the brand-new $10,000 toilet?" Gina said, ominously. "Of course you knew. Everyone knows."

Surely the woman hadn't taken a hammer to the toilet just because a worker had pissed in it?

"Look, it won't happen again. Just please, don't fire me. I need the job," the kid said, beseechingly.

Gina sniffed. "Sorry, you should have thought of that before," she snapped. "Now, get yourself over to the service elevator. You're done here!"

Charlotte dashed back to the spot where Gina had left her. As the blonde stepped towards her, she gave her a bright, innocent smile.

"Trouble with the help, Gina?"

"Sorry, Kate. But I couldn't help it. I wouldn't dream of using that toilet now! Not after he sat on it."

As they walked into the living room, Gina pointed at Charlotte's brand new green yoga mat.

"Hey! You really do take it with you everywhere, don't you?"

"I'd die without it!" Charlotte replied. "I have this teacher who's just amazing."

"Ashtanga?"

"Is there anything else?" Charlotte asked with a smile.

"I've tried a bit of iyengar, too," Gina added. "I love it. The last time I even flew my coach down with us to Mustique. We had the place just down the beach from Mick Jagger. Do you know the island?"

"No, I'm afraid I don't," Charlotte replied demurely.

"Well, we had them paint my bedroom a lovely muted shade of orange. Just like Madonna does when she travels. I find it really helps a lot with meditation and the stress of jet lag..."

"Right," said Charlotte, holding her mat and gazing in awe at the vast, loft-like space that had opened up in front of her. *OK, the woman is a monster*, thought Charlotte, *but how can I kill someone with style like this?*

While Gina traipsed off to get the silver, Charlotte inspected the room more closely. The colors were superb: sea grape lacquered walls, deep violet trims, Gaetano Pesce's tufted sofas, upholstered in jewel-tone satins, and flourishes of hot pink. Other nods to the "now" included a pair of low-slung slipper chairs in celery linen and a few very nice Paul Frankl deco pieces. A magnificent palace-size Kerman rug was thrown casually over the black-and-white-pinstripe-painted floor. She saw some Renaissance pieces that would have had Max drooling: two gilt and jewel-encrusted Italian Rococo mirrors and an embroidered stump work toilet box that had to be 16th century. There wasn't a single false note. Well, except for Gina.

"Do you like it?" the girl asked, setting down a brown wooden box on the rug.

"I think it's brilliant," Charlotte replied, honestly.

"A friend helped me," she said proudly. "'Let go and embrace what you really want!' he kept telling me."

"Well, your friend's a pro," Charlotte said, opening the box of silver. Gina sat down in a half lotus next to her as Charlotte ran her fingers over the monogram on a heavy fork.

"They were a wedding gift from my parents," she explained. "But Buccellati is so much nicer, don't you think?"

"I suppose so," Charlotte answered, replacing the fork in its slot. "I've never been married, of course. So…"

"Oh! I'm surprised," the girl said. "You're so attractive!"

Charlotte chuckled. "Marriage isn't the answer to everything, you know, Gina!"

"Don't tell me. I mean, I love Steve, don't get me wrong, we just disagree on some fundamental things."

"Really," said Charlotte, looking her in the eye. "Like what?"

"Well, like the fact I agreed to have a baby, but only if he promised me a boob job after! He wasn't happy, believe me. Steve's old, you know. He wanted more kids. But my breasts are one of my most valuable assets." she added, giving both of them a friendly pat.

"That's why I didn't nurse, either. The stretch marks on my stomach were bad enough."

I could strangle her right here and now, Charlotte thought. Instead she gave her the woman a hand and pulled her to her feet.

"Could we talk a little about price?" Charlotte asked, taking a seat on a nearby sofa.

"I suppose so," Gina replied sullenly. "But don't expect a big discount, Kate. It's never been used."

"I understand. And listen, I hate to put you out, but my yoga class was a two hour session today and I am parched."

"Oh, sorry! I've got some vitamin water right over here," Gina said, starting to cross the room. "I keep bottles everywhere around the house," she added, turning her back on Charlotte and walking towards the Regency sideboard.

Charlotte untied her mat.

"You really should try iyengar, Kate. I could give you the name of my coach," Gina chattered on. "It's helping me so much, handling all the preschool apps and stuff..."

"I'd love that," Charlotte replied, rising from her seat on the sofa. "Why don't I just take one more look at the silver? I'm not sure I like the idea of living with someone else's monograms."

"Fine!" Gina replied, holding the bottle and glass in one hand while squatting down to pick up a serving spoon.

The timing wasn't perfect but it would have to do. As Gina looked down, Charlotte walked slowly towards her, the poker hidden behind her back.

"What the ffff?" Gina yelped. Dropping the bottle, glass, and the spoon, she held her hands, palms out, to protect her face. Charlotte swooped down with the poker as the woman twisted her body away from the blow.

The poker sideswiped her head. Gina's knees buckled as she fell face first onto the carpet. The spoon lay in a small pool of blood next to her face.

"Ppllllease," Gina pleaded, one eye fixed on Charlotte's indifferent gaze. As Charlotte raised the poker, once more, a voice ripped through the room.

"Mommy! Mommy!"

Whipping around, Charlotte saw a small child standing near the doorway. He was looking right at her.

"What happened, Mommy? What happened?"

Charlotte froze. The echo of her own words on that long-ago morning paralyzed her. Gina was crawling forward on her elbows. Charlotte hesitated. *Kill her! Kill her now!* A voice inside shrieked. But she couldn't move. The child had started to howl. Putting her hands over her ears to block the sound, she shoved the monogrammed spoon into her pocket and dropped the poker. The howling was even louder. She could see tears streaming down the child's face.

Go! Charlotte, go! As the child began to walk towards his mother, Charlotte picked up the poker and staggered out into the vestibule. Her legs felt so heavy, as if they were running through deep water. Grabbing her coat, she pulled open the elevator door, ran inside, and punched "L" for lobby.

Fuck! she thought when it started its descent. *What if someone's waiting in the lobby? What if somebody gets in on another floor?* Sweat prickled at her neck as she desperately punched at the buttons.

41

Charlotte had no idea how long she'd been in the darkened bedroom or even how she'd gotten out of that elevator and into the house. She was just numb, so incredibly numb. *This is why girls cut themselves,* she thought, gnawing on her knuckles. S*o they can feel something.* All Charlotte ever felt was tired. So goddamn tired. She wondered if the pain of cutting made girls weep. Did they cry until they were weak and utterly spent? Of course, they didn't. Weeping was old-fashioned. It was all about control now, wasn't it? *Control, control, control.*

Hugging her knees, she felt the anger building again. It was almost a relief; as familiar as a loyal friend. Her mouth was dry and her eyes stung. Nothing seemed to erase the image of the child. She'd tried talking to her aunt, but Dottie wasn't there. She was alone, just as she'd always been alone. Twisting the latches behind the sterling silver picture frame, Charlotte carefully removed the photo, ran her fingers across its surface, and tore it into tiny pieces.

She felt as if she had bare-wired herself into a hot socket. Was the woman dead? Could the child give a description of her? Thank God her bright red hair had been hidden under her hat. She knew that she'd been inexcusably careless; that the police would lift her prints from the leather armrest of the living room couch, from the silver fork, and from the front doorknob. Of course, they wouldn't match her fingerprints. She wasn't in their database. She'd never been caught committing a crime. She didn't even have a driver's license. But if they found her otherwise...

Fists clenched, Charlotte pulled the eiderdown over her body and slipped two Ativans beneath her tongue. She'd have to leave town for a while. Just until things calmed down. Maybe she'd make the trip to Alpine. She could feel the warmth flow through her limbs as the pill dissolved. Charlotte closed her eyes and plunged into the oblivion of sleep.

42

It was hunger that finally forced Charlotte to confront the agony of bright light that flooded through the kitchen windows. Checking the gilded clock on the mantle, she saw that she'd been in her room for nearly forty hours. Pulling in the pile of newspapers that lay on the hallway floor, her heart hammered up against her chest. The story was splashed on the front cover of the previous morning's *Post*.

THE CRAIGSLIST MURDERS!

Ben Volpone

In what could be an astonishing break in the case of Amy Webb and other recent unsolved female homicides in Manhattan, a woman nearly bludgeoned to death in her Tribeca loft was left alive by her alleged attacker on Tuesday afternoon.

According to a Police Department spokeperson, "The victim, 27-year-old Gina Craven, is in intensive care at a local hospital. Doctors say her prognosis is good." Similar to other, less fortunate victims, Mrs. Craven suffered blunt trauma to the head.

For the first time since last April when Upper East divorcee, Judy Gross, was found dead in the living room of her apartment, police acknowledge a connection between Craigslist, the popular online shopping bazaar, and the murders of Mrs. Gross, Mrs. Webb, and Christina Johnson, a model killed in her Village brownstone last summer. As the police spokesperson confirms, "It appears that evidence now indicates that Craigslist is the method by which the perpetrator gained access into these victims' homes."

Unnamed sources within the department report that the victim's 4-year-old child was a witness to the attempted murder. As of late last evening, there was no news as to whether the mother or the child has yet helped the police identify or describe the attacker. The Police Commissioner will give a press conference on Friday morning at 9 a.m.

The victim, Gina Craven, is the third wife of renowned political pundit and "grape juice" billionaire, Timothy

Craven. Married five years ago in a beach ceremony on the Caribbean island of Mustique, Craven is a huge supporter of "Free Tibet" and a self-proclaimed good friend of the Dalai Lama.

Calls to Craig Newmark, the gnomish, iconoclastic founder of the list in San Francisco, were immediately referred back to the New York City Police Department. A man who answered the phone at the office, however, did mention that Craigslist had flagged a warning on its New York site several weeks ago, reminding users to "exercise the usual caution and common sense when dealing with unknown buyers and sellers." One of the hottest shopping sites online, Craigslist offers its users everything from antique furniture, clothing, and auto parts to sperm donors, and vintage Cabbage Patch dolls. With the possible exception of Mrs. Webb's brown Louis Vuitton vanity case, it is still not known what the other victims had offered for sale through Craigslist.

Charlotte sucked in a deep breath and sank down into a dining chair. The furious blinking on her message machine seemed to be in sync with her pulse rate. *Get a grip! Get a grip on yourself, Charlotte!* she whispered, popping the cap off a bottle of Ativan in the kitchen cabinet. As a rule, Charlotte avoided sedatives during the day, but she had to control the panic, to keep her stomach from cramping. Sliding the pill into her mouth, she chewed and pressed Play on her machine.

"Charlotte. It's Max. Somethin's up with your Russkie friend. His check bounced. Call me."

She trembled when she heard the next voice.

"Hey there, darling. Guess who? It's Philip. Listen, have you still got that bracelet from Craigslist? Call me."

Leaning in, she listened to the beginning of the next message and pressed Skip. It was some guy from accounting at Rosselli, probably about another bad check.

The next two messages left her wishing that she'd stayed in bed.

"Charlotte! It's Rita. Listen, I'm postponing our meeting about the new Vineyard House. So put the paint chips away. Abe says we're fine. Not to worry. I'll call you soon."

Then there was Darryl. "Hi! Do me a favor, will you. Cancel that order for the prison toilets and hold off on the dojo for Tim. I'm sure you'll understand, Charlotte. We're pulling back till this thing blows over."

Understand? Charlotte wailed to herself. *She can't pull back, not now. Not when I've already paid for the f'ing toilets.* Which was when her eyes tripped over the headline of Thursday's *Post.*

"DON'T LOOK DOW(N)!"

Her mind skittered around like a car on a patch of slick ice. The market had plunged 900 points overnight.

Christ! she thought. *It was bad enough being alone and broke. But being one among millions... Where the fuck was the comfort in that?*

Eyes pinned on phrases like "Uncertainty Spreads! Global Anxiety," Charlotte blindly grabbed the checkbook next to the answering machine and flipped through the tidily written sum, in search of her balance. Balance? There was no balance. She was running on fumes. Drying off her sweaty palms on a paper napkin, she struggled halfheartedly to make sense of it all.

Sure. There had been the collapse of Lehman Brothers and the fire sale at Merrill Lynch back in September. But neither had seemed to affect her clients. Subprime loans weren't exactly an issue for people building $50,000 swimming pools for their puggles, either. As for Fannie Mae and Freddie Mac… "They sound like country western singers!" is all Rita had said.

Hiding the checkbook under a pile of shelter magazines, Charlotte placed her palms on her temples and squeezed. Why, oh why, did the entire world have to panic and fall apart at the seams when she was scrambling so desperately to hold herself together and to fend off chaos? It was crazy.

Turning the pages of the Business section, she did find an uncanny irony in the news about a Wall Street crash. When was it she had first started her own personal crusade "cleaning house"? Had the gods finally heard her? Were they wreaking their own vengeance up there in her kill zone on the Upper East Side? Perhaps New York's trophy wives were about to become an even more endangered species.

She actually chuckled before pressing Play. There were three hang-ups and a woman's voice. It sounded tiny and distant.

"Charlotte. This is Lola. We've been trying to get you for two days. Your mother's had a series of small strokes. Call me in Alpine."

Charlotte hadn't spoken to her mother's housekeeper, Lola, in twenty years. They'd never liked each other. Even when she was a kid, the woman looked ancient—all hunched over and wrinkled. But maybe the strokes explained that strange moment when her mother had fumbled for words on her last visit? She shrugged. Not even strokes could excuse the cruelty of the gift. Charlotte began scratching at the bumps on her neck. The more she thought about her mother as an invalid, about taking care of her, about spending her own money (what money?) on nurses and doctors, the harder she scratched. In that last phone call, her mother had whined about feeling dizzy, light-headed.

Reaching for the phone, she picked up the receiver and speed-dialed home. *Home?* she sneered. *What home?* The bumps had spread from her neck to her chest. The itching was intolerable. The press conference on the murders was still thirty minutes away.

43

Hunkering down in the house, Charlotte drank cup after cup of neat espresso. Philip had left another message. But she hadn't returned his call. The Ativans had left a weird coppery taste in her mouth and her head felt leaden. When the newscaster on Channel 1 announced the beginning of the live press conference, she barely noticed when her Herend cup slipped from her fingers and crashed into pieces on the floor. Perched on the edge of her chair, she increased the volume and watched as the police commissioner took his place in front of a microphone. The mayor stood to his left along with several other men and a woman.

"Good morning, ladies and gentlemen. Thank you for coming. Just a word of warning before I bring you up to date on our investigation. I will not be taking any questions until after I have finished speaking. So please, do not interrupt me."

"As you are no doubt aware, Mrs. Gina Craven survived a vicious attack in her Tribeca loft on Tuesday afternoon and is currently in intensive care at Beth Israel Hospital. Doctors believe that she will make a full recovery but that she is in no condition for police questioning at this time..."

Charlotte could hear the buzz from reporters as the commissioner raised his hand for silence.

"I can tell you, however, that she was able to share a few significant details about her alleged attacker. Described as a female—"

An ear-splitting chorus of voices rose in the room as reporters leapt to their feet shouting, "Commissioner!" "Commissioner!"

"Sit! Sit!" the commissioner said in the firm no-nonsense voice used by dog trainers.

"Sit and I will finish. Otherwise..."

The reporters sat.

"As I was saying, the suspect is described as a Caucasian female with green eyes, between 5' 7" and 5' 10" tall and weighing approximately 130 pounds. She was last seen wearing black workout attire, a quilted black parka, a fur hat, and carrying a green yoga mat. A sketch of this suspect will be circulated around the city later this afternoon."

A reporter in the front row bolted to his feet.

The commissioner's command: "Heel, Ben, heel!" brought raucous laughter from the room. "What is it?"

"Sorry, commissioner. But half the women in this town walk around in workout attire, carrying yoga mats. What about the kid? Wasn't there a kid at the house?"

"The victim's son is four years old. He has just witnessed the attempted murder of his mother."

"Sorry, sorry!" came the flippant response from Ben Volpone. "But surely..."

"When the child's family determines that the he is ready to help, we will proceed. Next question," the commissioner added, making a point of ignoring Ben's wild arm-waving and nodding at a woman from the *Times*. "Go ahead, Jill."

"Thank you, sir. I'd like to ask about the Craigslist connection. Was Mrs. Craven selling something?"

"Yes, she had posted an ad for some Tiffany silver..."

"Can you tell us anything about the other victims? Do you have specific evidence or proof that links them with Craigslist and the attack on Mrs. Webb?"

"It's an ongoing investigation, Jill. So I'm not going to comment at length on that. Suffice it to say, there is a definite connection between Craigslist and the other murders. For more information, I'm sure the *Post*'s unnamed sources will be able to fill you in."

There were snorts of quiet laughter throughout the room.

The mayor took the mic. "I would just like to add that I am certain members of the press," he cast a laser-like stare at Ben Volpone, "will respect the family and the victim's need for privacy at this time."

Eager to have the last word, Volpone leapt to his feet. "Sir, sir! Why wasn't the public informed about the Craigslist connection, earlier? It might have saved..."

"We had posted our own ad, Ben. We were monitoring the site."

"Still..."

"No further questions," the mayor said, turning to the commissioner and touching his arm.

"I am sure you, Ben, join all of us in offering the family our heartfelt prayers for Mrs. Craven's speedy recovery. Thank you."

The remote reporter, tweaking his earphone, nodded at the anchorwoman on the screen. "Well, Joan, as you've just seen ... this is fairly astonishing news. Not just that there is a female serial killer loose on the streets of Manhattan, but that the killer is using a popular online shopping site to get into women's homes."

"It certainly is, Richard. Let's hope this reminds viewers to take extra special precautions when shopping or selling on the Internet. Just a quick question for you, Richard."

"Sure, Joan. Go ahead."

"Have you heard any talk down there about the housekeeper who called in with information after the killing of Amy Webb?"

"No, Joan. There was nothing said here. Maybe the police are waiting to locate the suspect before releasing her information. I'll try and follow up on that and get back to you."

"Thanks, Richard," said Joan, shifting to her left and addressing the camera. "And now we're switching to our health correspondent for some alarming news about the silent symptoms of female heart attacks."

Charlotte pushed the Off button on her remote control. Her cell phone was vibrating. Reading the caller ID, she recognized Vicky and Phil's home number. "No way!" she whispered as she stood up and walked towards her bedroom.

"Shit!" she shouted. Hopping around on the balls of her feet, she looked down at the trickle of blood. There was a shard of Herend porcelain embedded in her right heel. Plucking it out from her flesh, she wiped away her tears as blood gushed all over the freshly washed floor.

Twenty minutes later, her foot swathed in a homemade sock bandage, the phone vibrated again. It was her car service. Charlotte limped out of the apartment.

44

As the Town Car sped up the West Side Highway towards the hospital, she struggled to control her heart palpitations. She was having trouble breathing. Charlotte was used to instilling fear in *others*. This fear was different. It sat on her like a swelteringly hot and humid summer day, soaking into her pores and hanging heavy on her skin. It clutched her in the belly. The close call with Gina, the press conference, the news about her mother... It all seemed irrelevant, somehow. God! Where was Anna when she needed her?

If her clients suddenly tightened their belts, Charlotte would be out of business. Between the anorexic five grand left in the Caymans account that Abe had opened for her and an exhausted credit line, she'd be bankrupt. Then what the hell would she do? Work as a cashier at D'Agostino? A sales clerk at Barnes & Noble? It was surreal, she thought, gazing out at the river traffic on the Hudson where nothing appeared to have changed.

Unlike the day when the towers fell, this crash was

invisible. You couldn't see it. Or feel it or smell it. For a moment that felt as brief as a blink, she remembered those weeks after 9/11. The layers of soot and ash that lay like snow on the streets, that cushioned every footstep and created a world of startling soundlessness. There had been no traffic downtown. The normal noises of the city simply ceased to exist. No sirens or shouts, no trucks making deliveries or cabs, no horns. It was like some eerie homage to the dead, that stillness, the silence. As the car pulled up on the corner of West 180th and Broadway, Charlotte took a calming breath. It was sinister, this medieval, fortress-like building. Maybe it wasn't too late to turn around? *Breathe, Charlotte. Inhale,* she murmured to herself. Standing still, she waited quietly until her heart slowed. Pulling her phone out from the pocket of her Burberry jacket, she speed-dialed Dr. Greene. Expecting a machine, his voice surprised her and she hung up. As the revolving doors whisked her into the lobby, she headed towards an empty elevator.

After a talk with the nurses in the corridor, Charlotte stepped towards the door of her mother's private room. The nurses had informed her that the strokes had started months earlier, and that they had affected her memory. "The beginnings of a mild dementia, dear," they said. "But rehab can work miracles. So we'll just have to wait and see." Charlotte opened and quietly closed the door behind her. Nothing prepared her for the sight of the shrunken husk that lay on the clean white bed. Everything about her mother had been diminished. This beautiful, untouchable woman in whose shadow Charlotte had struggled to breathe for so many years, to find light, to feel love, was gone. The right side of her mouth and one eye were drooping. The impeccably maintained head of hair was knotted and greasy. She was almost unrecognizable.

"Hello, Mother," Charlotte whispered. The baleful stare only made Charlotte smile. "How are you feeling?" Dumping her coat on a chair, she kept one hand on the doorknob and sat down.

The woman in the bed made a feeble attempt to turn her head as Charlotte resumed speaking, making no effort to approach her.

"You know, I came up here with the idea of hurting you, she whispered. "Physically, I mean. But I don't really see how I could inflict much more damage than this, do you?" Pulling out her silver compact from her bag, Charlotte took three steps towards the bed and placed the mirror directly in front of her mother's one good eye. Her left hand flailed around beneath the sheet as she moaned.

"Ugly and useless, Mother. Do you remember telling me that? And do you remember sending me that lovely gift?" she asked, retreating back to the chair near the door. The only response was a blank stare.

Arranging her coat so it hung neatly in the chair back behind her, Charlotte crossed her knees and began to talk. "Do you know there was a time when I loved you, Mother? When I wanted to grow up and be just like you? I wanted pretty clothes and a pretty house."

As Charlotte moved into the rhythm of her words, her

eyes wandered towards the window and her voice assumed a dreamlike tone. A heavy sigh from her mother interrupted her.

"Am I boring you, Mother?" she said. "Because this is when the story gets interesting. Anyway, as it turns out, I grew up to be just like you. I learned to smile, Mother. I acquired style. Great style. And now there are just a few minor differences between the two of us."

Digging down into her bag, Charlotte removed the *Post* and set it on her lap.

"For instance, I decided to do something with my anger, Mother. To make the world a better place! So I've been getting rid of women like you. Women with a social conscience, *social* being the operative word. Ah! I see you've opened your eyes. But you can't read, can you? I'll help you." Pointing to the headline, Charlotte read the words "The Craigslist Murders" out loud.

Then her eyes drifted back towards the window and she spoke, almost wistfully. "You can't imagine how it feels, Mother. It's like soaring, *flying*, that moment when the poker hits flesh. I'm so alive, so connected to these women. Even my pores feel as if they're absorbing their life force. I'm releasing them, you see? That's what they don't understand. They should be grateful to me."

Seeing her mother's scrawny fingers fumbling towards the call button, Charlotte just smiled.

"I made a mistake, this time. I left a woman alive. The papers call her a *victim*. But she isn't a victim, Mother. She's a predator. Just like all the other women I've released from their misery. Women, like you, who know the price of everything but the cost of nothing. You and all your exquisite beautiful things," Charlotte whispered. "Everything you touch is precious. But you live in emotional squalor. Are you listening, Mother?"

Her mother was watching Charlotte's every move with one good eye and fidgeting around with her fingers.

"Just the thought of you living in such pain gives me pleasure, Mother. Because you don't deserve to die. Letting you live is a perfect punishment."

Hearing a discreet tap on the door, Charlotte turned around, and gave the nurse her most radiant smile.

"Oh nurse. I'm so glad to see you," she said. "My mother can't seem to stop crying."

"Don't worry about it too much," the nurse replied. "Stroke victims often cry."

"Oh! What a relief, nurse. I've been sitting here talking about my favorite childhood memories, hoping they might cheer her up."

"Has she been angry, too?" the nurse asked, patting Charlotte's mother on the hand. "Anger is also very common after strokes."

Charlotte gave her mother a saintly smile. "My mother's never angry, nurse. That's what makes her so easy to love," she said, giving her a kiss on the forehead.

"I have to leave now, unfortunately. But I'll be back up, tomorrow, Mother," Charlotte said, giving her a sympathetic nod and strolling towards the door.

"We'll take very good care of her tonight, I promise," the nurse said, straightening out the tangle of sheets.

Thanking her for her patience, Charlotte calmly walked out into the corridor and sighed. She would go home, pack a bag, and take a train somewhere. Anywhere. She needed time to plan her next move. As the elevator doors whooshed close, the nurse scurried down the corridor. "Miss! Your coat! You forgot your coat!"

45

Christ, she was uncomfortable. The metal springs in the cab seat were poking through the leather. She could barely sit still. Fiddling with her seatbelt, she leaned forward and ordered the driver to get off the West Side Highway. It was cold out. And she'd forgotten her goddamn coat. Christ! And her cell phone. How could there be so much traffic at this hour? These people were supposed to be leaving, not coming into town. The driver was praying or something. They just sat there, going nowhere.

Charlotte closed her eyes and tried to sing. The notes stuck like dry cotton in her throat. The horns, the stopping and starting, were driving her crazy. Glancing at her watch as the cab snaked its way past a bus on 34th Street and turned down 9th Avenue, she wondered if police had circulated the sketch of the attacker. And what about the calls from Philip? He knew. She was sure he knew. But had he called the cops?

Looking impatiently out the window, Charlotte unbuckled her belt and told the driver to stop. He'd turned off 9th Avenue and made it down to 7th and Carmine Street. The Holland Tunnel was slowing them down again. She'd power walk the rest of the way.

The accident happened so fast, she had no time to react.

She heard the shriek of horns before the thud. Her head crashed up against the partition and she blacked out. When she opened her eyes, her vision was fuzzy, smeared like a windshield pelted by rain. Rubbing her eyes, she saw the blue cloth of his uniform first.

"Miss, miss," he said, sticking his head through the passenger window. "Are you alright? Can you hear me?" Deliberately pushing her hair in front of her face, she nodded.

"I'm fine, officer. A little shook up but fine."

"An ambulance is on the way. Just sit tight."

Feeling gingerly around beneath her hair with her fingertips, she winced. The bump was enormous. It was bleeding. She could hear the shrill whine of an ambulance in the distance. She had to move, quickly. The cabbies were screeching at one another in Urdu when the punching started and the cop edged his way towards the curb. Charlotte slid slowly across the seat. If she could only get out of the cab, the crowd would swallow her. She could disappear. Her stomach was churning. Just as she pulled the door handle, the cop turned around and stared at her. He squinted. She gave him a weak smile and waved. When he turned his back on her, Charlotte calmly opened the door and walked into the crowd.

"Hey, lady, where are you going?" some guy yelled. "You're hurt!"

Keeping her head down, Charlotte moved at a funereal pace. The impulse to run was almost irresistible. Tensed and waiting for that sickening lurch when the cop would grab her shoulder and stop her, she started to hum.

Sticking close to the side of buildings, she walked along Carmine Street and took a right on Downing. The cop and cabbies were now out of sight. Shivering, she broke into a jog. Fifteen minutes later, Charlotte was so hot, she'd pulled off her sweater and tied it around her waist. Taking a fast right, she hurried down North Moore towards the safety of home.

John was heading straight for her.

God! Not now, John! Not now! she muttered as he blocked her way. "I'm in a rush, John. I'll give you something, later, I promise," she said, pushing to get past him.

"Charlotte! Charlotte!" He whispered. "Police. Police!"

She stopped, nailed to the spot, as he shuffled around on his feet, his eyes flitting up and down the block.

"Calm down, John," she said, soothingly. "What do you mean, police?"

"Don't know. Don't know. They're in your building. They're after me."

Charlotte forced herself to breathe. "How long have they been there, John?"

He was rifling through his shopping bag.

"How many of them?" Charlotte asked, gently resting her hand on his arm.

"A few, Charlotte. A few..."

"Well, I'm sure they're not after you. But I'll talk to them, okay? I'll tell them we're friends.

He nodded.

"Here," Charlotte said, pulling out a twenty dollar bill. "Buy yourself some cigarettes. It's going to be okay, I swear."

"Thanks, Charlotte. Thanks!"

Watching him head towards the Korean market, Charlotte turned around and began to walk towards SoHo. She thought about the fantasies she'd had after seeing Pavel, about his tattoo of the sailing ship and his talk of freedom. She also thought about how tired she had grown of her tiny, incestuous world in New York. She longed for the terror and the challenge of new beginnings. Thinking of Pavel and his banya, she imagined plunging into a river of cool rushing water. A burst of adrenaline surged through her veins as she stepped up her pace and looked up at a sapphire-blue sky. For the first time in years, Charlotte felt almost light on her feet—untethered. Like one of those big bright-striped hot air balloons that, once freed of the weights and the ropes that lash them to the ground, drift ever so slowly, up and into the air.

CRAIGSLIST MURDERER ELUDES COPS!

By Ben Volpone

In a story that only grows stranger and more complicated over time, police informed the media this morning that they have identified a "person of interest" in the attack on Gina Craven. "We would like to talk with her, ask a few questions, is all," said the spokesperson. Although sources refused to cite her as a probable suspect, her name is Charlotte Wolfe.

Admired for her interior design work by the wives of the city's richest, most powerful financial wizards, Ms. Wolfe lives in a downtown Tribeca loft where police were waiting to question her yesterday evening after receiving a call from her Greenwich Village psychiatrist. Unfortunately, Wolfe has yet to show up and police now fear that she may have been warned and left the city.

Reluctant to disclose the exact nature of the

psychiatrist's concern, sources close to the investigation did reveal that it involved a recorded cell phone conversation and the possibility of bodily assault. "It seems this person accidentally speed-dialed her doctor. And an emergency exception allowed police to enter the premises of the phone registered to the patient in question." The source also disclosed that it was only after police had entered the premises that a possible connection was made between Wolfe and the Craigslist murders. "A detective on the case recognized several pieces of evidence, including a monogrammed silver spoon, at which point a search warrant was issued. It appears that there is other evidence also links Wolfe to the killings of Amy Webb and Christina Johnson."

Described by Rita Brickman, a shocked longtime friend and client, as "both lovely and immensely talented," Wolfe began her career working as an assistant to the celebrated late designer Harold Beamish. When asked to comment on the news about Wolfe, Beamish's partner, Miles van den Broek, hardly minced words. "We called her the 'halo from hell,'" he said. "Nothing about her would surprise me."

In an exclusive interview, Philip Daft, a client of Wolfe's and one of New York's most respected philanthropists, mentioned that he had actually seen the suspect wearing what is now suspected to be a piece of evidence. "It was a gold charm bracelet," he said, speaking from the street on his way into the Union Club. "I noticed it right away, because my wife wanted one. I remember Charlotte told me she'd bought it on Craigslist. I was shocked. It's not the sort of thing you hear from our people." As he approached the door of the club, Mr. Daft turned around.

"Of course, Charlotte was never really our people." Follow-up calls to his wife, a close friend of the suspect, were not returned.

The daughter of Millicent Connors and Benjamin Wolfe, Charlotte Wolfe was brought up on in one of New York's most exclusive Fifth Avenue buildings. She attended the elite Chapin School and Sarah Lawrence College. Police request anyone with information about her whereabouts to contact 1-800-577-TIPS immediately.

46

EIGHTEEN MONTHS LATER

Entering the trustees' dining room at the Cincinnati Museum of Art, she was greeted by the sound of muted but heartfelt applause. Lowering her emerald green eyes, she smiled, and gave her husband's arm a gentle squeeze. Everyone affectionately called her Bet. With her champagne-streaked blonde hair pulled back in a sleek, tight chignon, her statuesque build, sun-kissed skin, and ruby red lips, people said she looked a lot like an older version of Carolyn Bessette. Had she lived, of course. The poor thing.

Yes, the women in town all agreed that she'd had some work done: the forehead, the creases between her nose and mouth, maybe even a discreet lift to the eyes. But it was so subtle, it only added to her allure. This was just one of the extraordinary things about Bet. Women envied her, but they also loved being near her. Every charity event in town that she sponsored was wildly oversubscribed. And no one ever turned down an invitation to one of her marvelous dinners at home or a weekend in the country.

The other extraordinary thing about Bet was her marriage to George. George's mother had been a gorgon—an absolute harridan. When Bet arrived in town out of nowhere, with no credentials to speak of, no background, no real money, everyone at the club had given her relationship with George a month, two at the most. After all, they'd witnessed the social demise of so many other younger, wealthier, more suitable women.

But Bet had not only succeeded in defanging George's mother, she'd befriended her, too. In fact, Bet's friends were convinced that it was her tireless nursing and infinite patience before the old woman's unexpected but merciful demise that cinched the couple's marriage. She and George had been virtually inseparable ever since.

Last but far from least, was Bet's style. You could forgive a woman almost anything, including a somewhat dubious past, when she had style like Bet. It wasn't just the way she dressed or what she'd done with the house. It was how modest and generous she was with other women. Everybody had called her in at one point or another for advice. Whether it involved a decision as mundane as choosing a color for the new maid's room or as important as decorating a nursery for the baby, or buying some hugely expensive piece of French furniture at auction, Bet just *knew*.

What was it she had given all the girls at Christmas? Fabulous eighteen-karat gold straight pins in velvet boxes? "So you can tell the fake from the real thing," she'd said in her notes, after thanking them for making her feel at home in Cincinnati.

The party at the museum had gone on till two a.m. After making love to his wife, George fell asleep. She had waited until she heard the sound of his snoring before creeping into her dressing room and locking the door behind her. She was exhausted, wrung out. Eight hours of vapid, small talk with such boring, tedious women. One more story about an adorable eight-year-old Mozart prodigy and she thought was going to puke. Did they ever talk about anything but their children? Stripping down to her $1,000 Nina Ricci bra and thong, she smoothed the creases out of the Dior dress and carefully hung it up in its proper place.

At first, her husband had objected to the idea of seven custom-made closets. "Dear God, darling," he'd stammered over his second bourbon old-fashioned. "This is a recession, we're in! No woman in Cincinnati needs seven closets!" But just like his objections to the Toto toilet (which he now admitted was a pretty "neat" invention), he had eventually surrendered.

She was working on the jet now. She'd launched her campaign during their honeymoon in Europe. George had fumed at every airport as they trekked through endless lines and waited to board delayed flights. (He had insisted on flying American carriers only. "It's patriotic, darling," he'd said. "The least we can do, you know?") But American flights were notoriously late. Seated in their first class seats, he'd also complained about the service. "What the hell happened to those young, smiling stewardesses?" he'd blustered. "It's worse than fucking Aeroflot." George never swore.

He was the only child of one of Ohio's richest families, old-fashioned American industrialists. Unlike Vicky and Phil Phil whose fortune had dwindled and shrunk to next to nothing during the cataclysmic ups and downs of the real estate market (and how Charlotte had gloated over that delicious bit of news in the *New York Times*), George had always been cautious with his money. He was so cautious he had modestly confided that his own portfolio was down a mere 15% percent. Nevertheless, even when they'd been bumped off a flight from Paris to Rome, he'd said that a jet was simply out of the question.

"It's so showy, darling. So conspicuous. And the fuel costs! Good lord! We'd be busted."

She'd had wanted to kill Laurie and Ned when they'd come over for dinner and tittered about last summer's $12,000 NetJets fare from New York to Nantucket. She, of course, had no interest in NetJets.

What was it Vicky had said to her after she and Philip had flown to Paris for the first time on the G-5? "Listen, darling. I don't mind sharing my feelings. But I'm sure as hell not going to share my jet!" Charlotte giggled at the memory. Their jet was probably gathering dust in some hangar at Teterboro with a for sale sign plastered on the cockpit window. George could pick it up for a song. *And wouldn't that just be perfect poetic justice?* she thought. Zipping around the skies in Vicky's favorite travel toy?

Last week, she'd surprised George at breakfast with the catalogue from Gulfstream instead. "It's just for fun, darling," she'd said. "To see how the other half of one percent lives." She then began to skim through the Styles section in the Sunday *Times*.

Actually, she called it the *smiles* section. On one exceedingly boring Sunday morning, she'd counted the number of smiles per page. When she got to 74 and realized she was only on page eight, she'd quit. That was when she'd also seen the photo of Anna and Pavel, holding hands at a benefit for the Costume Institute. The taste of bile rose in her throat as she crumpled up the newspaper.

Unlike others who subscribed to the *Times* in far-flung cities, she knew that the socialites pictured had nothing to smile about. They were all either discreetly addicted to antidepressants and painkillers and locking themselves into panic rooms to scream and cry or flat broke.

Stranded here in Cinci and seeing that photo of Rita hiding under a baseball cap and visiting Abe down at the Tombs had her laughing so hard, George had come galloping in from the library to thump her on the back. My God! Genial, affable Abe. The biggest swindler of all time. The kind of sweet old Jewish man everybody wished was their grandfather. It was unbelievable.

Standing sideways in front of the mirror, she grinned at her reflection and ran her hands over the small bump in her belly. She tried to forget the slobbering wet kiss that she'd had to endure when she gave George the news. The pregnancy had been his biggest birthday surprise. When the cramps had started again, she'd seen a local gynecologist. The sonogram of her abdomen had been quite a revelation. Not only did she have gallstones ("You've probably had them for years," the doctor had told her) and two large cysts on her right ovary (one of which had resolved itself), she was also three months pregnant.

Sighing, she dumped her underwear in the hamper,

spritzed her blonde hair with a mist of Joy (*That's right, Joy,* she thought. Her mother's own signature scent.) and played her old "what if" game. What if she hadn't left her coat and cell phone in the hospital? What if she hadn't run into John on the street? What if Abe hadn't opened that small starter fund for her in the Caymans? Five grand wasn't much but it had been just enough to cover her getaway. She remembered how her shrink used to laugh at her for reading the *Post*, too. Poor Dr. Greene. She wondered if he'd ever forgive himself for turning her in after overhearing her confession on the cellphone. Anyway, after reading that piece in the *Post* about the business of identity theft in the Baja, it had cost her a measly $2,000 to become Elizabeth Gordon. Bet, for short. The rest: the work on her face in L.A., the hair, even the switch involved in becoming a perfect trophy wife, had been easy.

There were moments, in fact, when it was so easy, when the role felt so remarkably *natural*, she caught herself wondering who she really was. A week ago, she'd started trawling through the List, again. Just for fun, of course. But still... It was amazing. The kind of stuff women were selling off during the recession! And they were the lucky ones. George had caught Charlotte chortling in bed one morning. She had been reading Page Six, a paragraph about men trudging into Madison Avenue boutiques with shopping bags. It seems they were returning everything their wives had bought that still had a price tag on it and pocketing the cash. *Tough times*, Charlotte thought, as she smiled and slipped into a peach silk dressing gown.

THANKS

To the seventy-eight editors/publishers who turned this novel down. Without them, I might never have found such a happy home at Melville House. Thanks also to the believers, to those whose faith (blind as it might have seemed) kept me hoping… To the Almighty Wolcott (a/k/a James) and Laura Jacobs, writer and friend extraordinaire. To the agent, Yfat Reiss Gendell, who took this book on as her very first project at Foundry Media and whose phenomenal success since has had nothing to do with me. To Brendan Bernhard who opened the door at Melville and my sister, Rachel, and reader Akiko Busch, both of whom loved Charlotte even in her fetal stages. Last but hardly least… Huge thanks to my husband, Richard, and to Jack and Nora who lived with a murderous mother for as long as it took to get Charlotte, her fire poker, and her yoga mat out there.